Author's Not

From The Library Of
BARBARA L. OLSON

When my editor told r
month of **TREASURE**
wanted to do—*The Phantom of the Opera.* My phantom, Jonathan, had to be a scarred man who's lost the capacity to love and has hidden himself from the world, not because he is disfigured, but because he is punishing himself.

My beautiful, innocent heroine, Shannon, had to be scarred as well, not physically but emotionally. Together they had to learn that love is the magic that brings joy to life.

Their lives have, in different ways, become the kind of illusion that the original phantom created, filled with loneliness, dark places, and mazes from which they can't escape.

To give my phantom the freedom to love again, his darkness had to be balanced against the magic of love. Who better to bring magic into his life than a shy fairy who has found a different way to hide from life's dark moments.

My setting had to be a magic mountain, during the most magical time of year, Christmas. The catalyst that brings them together had to be a child who has lost her belief in Santa Claus. With these ingredients, a sensual, magical story, *Night Dreams,* was born.

Dear reader, I hope that you'll forgive the freedom I've taken with Gaston Leroux's haunting story, *The Phantom of the Opera.* I always wanted Erik to find love. I've created my own illusion in retelling this classic tale. I hope you'll find it worthy of the spirit of the season in which it's being offered.

Sandra Chastain

WHAT ARE *LOVESWEPT* ROMANCES?

They are stories of true romance and touching emotion. We believe those two very important ingredients are constants in our highly sensual and very believable stories in the *LOVESWEPT* line. Our goal is to give you, the reader, stories of consistently high quality that may sometimes make you laugh, sometimes make you cry, but are always fresh and creative and contain many delightful surprises within their pages.

Most romance fans read an enormous number of books. Those they truly love, they keep. Others may be traded with friends and soon forgotten. We hope that each *LOVESWEPT* romance will be a treasure—a "keeper." We will always try to publish

LOVE STORIES YOU'LL NEVER FORGET
BY AUTHORS YOU'LL ALWAYS REMEMBER

The Editors

Sandra Chastain

Night Dreams

BANTAM BOOKS
NEW YORK · TORONTO · LONDON · SYDNEY · AUCKLAND

NIGHT DREAMS
A Bantam Book / January 1993

LOVESWEPT® and the wave design are registered trademarks of Bantam Books, a division of Bantam Doubleday Dell Publishing Group, Inc. Registered in U.S. Patent and Trademark Office and elsewhere.

All rights reserved.
Copyright © 1992 by Sandra Chastain.
Cover art copyright © 1992 by Mort Engel.
No part of this book may be reproduced or transmitted in any form or by any means, electronic or mechanical, including photocopying, recording, or by any information storage and retrieval system, without permission in writing from the publisher.
For information address: Bantam Books.

If you purchased this book without a cover you should be aware that this book is stolen property. It was reported as "unsold and destroyed" to the publisher and neither the author nor the publisher has received any payment for this "stripped book."

If you would be interested in receiving protective vinyl covers for your Loveswept books, please write to this address for information:

Loveswept
Bantam Books
P.O. Box 985
Hicksville, NY 11802

ISBN 0-553-44270-8

Published simultaneously in the United States and Canada

Bantam Books are published by Bantam Books, a division of Bantam Doubleday Dell Publishing Group, Inc. Its trademark, consisting of the words "Bantam Books" and the portrayal of a rooster, is Registered in U.S. Patent and Trademark Office and in other countries. Marca Registrada. Bantam Books, 666 Fifth Avenue, New York, New York 10103.

PRINTED IN THE UNITED STATES OF AMERICA

OPM 0 9 8 7 6 5 4 3 2 1

For my own real live Kaseybelle—my daughter, Kim, who brings the magic of imagination into all our lives.

And for Susann Brailey, my editor, who knows the special joy of being the mother of her own little girl, Tara.

One

At the top of the mountain the castle loomed black against the moon, like a pen-and-ink drawing of the majestic Paris Opera House on a theater program.

Shannon didn't know what she'd expected of Jonathan Dream's hideaway, searchlights and dancing girls, perhaps, certainly not the eerie splendor of turrets against the North Carolina sky.

The snow swirled outside the limo window. It seemed an eternity had passed as they climbed steadily, rounding curving mountain roads in silence. She had begun to feel like a woman in some Gothic novel. There was even an iron gate that had to be unlocked, and locked again once they entered.

It was no place for Shannon Summers, shy advertising artist, to be. And she wouldn't have been there if it hadn't been for Kaseybelle and the Kissy Chocolate Company. The threat of seeing her dearest friend hurt had forced her to answer Jonathan Dream's summons.

Moments later the limo came to a stop. "Don't let the building get to you, Ms. Summers," the driver said as he helped her out of the car.

There wasn't even a Christmas wreath on the door to welcome them. "Why would anyone build such a place up here?" she asked.

"The castle was started in the twenties by a nostalgic Frenchman who eventually lost everything in the Depression. Jonathan only finished it."

The driver carried her overnight bag into the brightly lit foyer and up the grand staircase.

"All Mr. Dream needs are a few sword-bearing members of the Garde Républicaine wearing white buckskin trousers and helmets and standing at attention," Shannon stated.

"I see you know about the real Place de l'Opéra."

"Yes, and I've seen Andrew Lloyd Webber's play and read the book from which it was adapted."

Shannon was overwhelmed by the grandeur of the second-floor gallery, complete with arches and marble. It literally could have been copied from the Paris Opera House. Willie hadn't prepared her for this.

"Shame on you, Lawrence." A small, gray-haired woman appeared from the other end of the gallery. She took the bag and gave the driver a frown. "This poor girl looks frozen. Come along, Miss Summers. You have the tower suite." She darted to her right and up a smaller set of circular stairs to the top of the tower, where she pushed open the door to a room that filled the entire turret.

"I'm Mrs. Butter. Well, not really. My name is Butterfield, but DeeDee shortened it to Butter and that's what everyone calls me now. You must be hungry. I can't imagine why Mr. Jonathan didn't get you a flight that arrived at a decent hour."

"Neither can I," Shannon said under her breath as she tried to restore some kind of order to a mass of fine blond hair that defied control.

"I've already laid out a carafe of hot cocoa and a plate of sandwiches. If you need anything else, just ask."

Shannon might have asked where Mr. Dream was, if she'd been given a chance. But short of blowing a time-out whistle, Shannon could see that she wasn't going to be able to interrupt.

Mrs. Butter plumped up the pillows, laid Shannon's case on the bed, and unfastened it. "I'll just put away your things. Lawrence will be up with the rest of your luggage shortly."

"There is no more luggage," Shannon said softly, overwhelmed by the motherly, take-charge manner of the woman who appeared to be the housekeeper.

"But surely you brought—I mean, you'll be needing more than just a nightgown, won't you. Mr. Dream said you'd be here for—some time."

"He did? Well, he's mistaken. I came, but I can't stay. I'll only be here the night."

"Never mind. I suppose it won't matter. He'll supply whatever you need. He always keeps the drawers stocked with lingerie for guests even if we don't have many outsiders anymore. There was a time when—well, never mind. We're going to enjoy having you here. You'll find sleepwear in the bureau."

"I brought my own sleepwear."

Mrs. Butter held up Shannon's pink flannel nightgown and smiled. "That you did. And sensible sleepwear it is, not at all what I expected. Well, if there's nothing else you need, I'll leave you now."

"There is one thing," Shannon said, stopping the housekeeper in the doorway. "Does Mr. Dream play an organ?"

Mrs. Butterfield looked confused as she answered.

"Play an organ? Not Jonathan. Goodness, no. And his name's really Jonathan Drew. He just calls himself Jonathan Dream because of those clothes he sells. He said to tell you that he'll see you tomorrow. You have a snack and get a good night's sleep. And in the morning you'll meet DeeDee. She's going to love you. Oh, yes. I think you're going to do just fine. Good night."

She was leaving. The only welcoming note Shannon had seen since she'd left Atlanta was closing the door and leaving her. "Wait!"

But she was already gone.

"Phoo on you, too, Willie Hicks!" Shannon said as she slammed the door and clicked the lock. "If you weren't my boss and if I didn't totally adore you, I'd mail you a letter bomb and completely obliterate the offices of Expressions Advertising from Atlanta, Georgia's, famous Peachtree Street.

No, she wouldn't. She couldn't refuse Willie. For she owed Willie everything. Even the television company producing the Kaseybelle Kartoons couldn't believe that she elected to stay with Willie rather than join their production staff.

If if hadn't been for Willie, Shannon Summers, the little-known daughter of the late screen star, Sofia Summers, would still be an introverted art student. And Kaseybelle would still be her imaginary childhood playmate instead of the trademark for Kissy Chocolates.

It was Jonathan Dream she ought to be blaming. He was the one who'd coerced her into coming by promising Willie a multimillion-dollar advertising account if Shannon represented the firm in person.

Jonathan Dream. Every supermarket tabloid was fascinated by the story of the former international playboy, owner of NightDreams Lingerie, who six years earlier had turned into a mysterious recluse. And every newspaper gave its own fictitious account of the reason why. He'd lost his mind. He'd contracted some terrible disease. He'd developed a people phobia and refused to leave the house.

Idly, Shannon glanced around, wondering if anyone knew the truth. She might complain about her travel schedule, but she couldn't complain about her room. It was bathed in a soft golden light that fell from somewhere beneath the molding along the lower edge of the ceiling. Though the wind whistled against the brick turret, she felt as if she were being infused with warmth.

A canopy bed, draped with gauzy hangings, filled a section of the curved wall. Several large, undraped windows made squares of charcoal on either side of a door framing the darkness and the moon.

On the wall beside the door they'd entered, Shannon found a knob that dimmed the lights almost to darkness. Now she could see the balcony outside, and the huge evergreen trees with their limbs drooping gracefully to the ground from the weight of the snow. Though it was only late November, winter had come to the Carolina mountains.

Moonlight turned the view from her window into an early Christmas card, reminding Shannon of the time she'd accompanied Sofia to Austria. It must have been the winter before her mother had married the count who had become husband number three. The snow there had been deep and white and scary to a child. Only Kaseybelle had understood Shannon's fear. Only Kaseybelle had been there to comfort her when her mother had grown tired of trying to amuse the child she barely knew and abandoned her to a staff who hardly spoke English.

Now another self-centered celebrity was doing the same thing, taking her someplace she didn't want to go and abandoning her. Except now she was an adult.

Shannon peered down the mountainside. There was movement, a wild animal perhaps. Only a flitting smear of shadow on the white, then nothing. There, she saw it again. Intrigued, she opened the door and stepped outside into the icy night.

Folding her arms across her chest, she stood, rubbing herself vigorously as she watched. There was something eerie about the quiet, broken only occasionally by a plop of falling snow. Then she saw him, the man standing at the edge of the precipice. Dressed in some kind of boots and a thick jacket, he was very tall and so still that she could see the little puffs of frosty air making a halo around him when he breathed.

In the moonlight he was simply a silhouette against the snow, a dark apparition. Yet there was a tension in his stance, a stance that suggested he wore the weight of loneliness like a heavy cloak. For a long time he stood without moving, then he turned and looked up at the house, catching her in the potency of his gaze.

She couldn't see his eyes. She couldn't even see his face. All she saw was a shape that suggested long hair and the lean, hungry look of a predator. She should have been apprehensive, but she wasn't. A sensation of danger mixed with anticipation jabbed her nerve endings like Morse code. Shannon's breath quickened and she took an involuntary step backward.

If he was Jonathan Dream, she could believe all the tales of ruthless persistence, of power and success. Even from across a courtyard, the connection between them was so intense that she could feel the breathless skip of her heart. It had to be the setting, not the man that mesmerized her. But as she stood, she could almost hear him call out to her. And her lips parted to answer.

Shannon whirled around and darted back inside to escape the overwhelming sensation. She'd take care of her business first thing in the morning and go home. If she'd wanted to live her life on the edge, taking on the world of the rich and famous, she'd have done so long ago.

Her simple little life at the advertising agency was exactly what she wanted. It was comfortable, pleasant, and she had no intention of leaving it for anybody, certainly not a man who didn't even show her the courtesy of a personal welcome. No, she didn't owe him more than a brief explanation that she was not the person to discuss his advertising campaign. She only worked with the Kissy Chocolate Company. He'd made a mistake in demanding that she represent Expressions Advertising.

Shannon pulled out Kaseybelle, the look-alike

fairy doll she'd designed and brought to life as the trademark for Kissy Chocolates, and studied her creation. The doll she held had been the prototype and had been hugged so often that it was beginning to fray around the edges.

She let out a deep breath and poured herself a cup of the hot cocoa. With the sweet liquid she ate one of Mrs. Butter's sandwiches, forcing herself to override the pull that drew her back to the window. Whoever the man outside was, he was a threat—not physically, for Mrs. Butter had told her she had nothing to fear, but on some deeper level.

No, it was more than that. Shannon had the feeling that coming to this place would unsettle her in a different way. And she already knew change in her life was to be avoided. When things changed, she lost control, and it had taken her most of her life to gain it.

Quickly Shannon removed her suede skirt and boots, donned her pink flannel nightgown, and slid under the covers. She'd leave the lights on dim. "Kaseybelle would like that," she whispered, tucking the doll into the curve of her arm, and the fairy she represented into the secret part of her mind, where Shannon had kept her as a child.

From somewhere in the house the deep, melodic chime of a grandfather clock announced the hour.

Midnight. No time for an interview anyway. Neither was it time for a stroll in the moonlight. Except the man hadn't been strolling. He'd been waiting.

Waiting?

Shannon closed her eyes and forced herself to think of the story treatment she was working on for the television program that Kissy Chocolate sponsored. She'd suggest an episode where Kaseybelle spent the night in a strange castle. The television writers would do the actual script. Shannon only did the advertising art and assisted in creating Kaseybelle's adventures.

Kaseybelle would wish she were back home, Shannon thought, where she'd be safe. Just as she was falling asleep, she remembered Mrs. Butter's words: "In the morning you'll meet DeeDee." Shannon wondered who DeeDee was.

Jonathan had known she was there before he'd turned and seen her watching him. For a moment he'd been tempted to cover his face, then he'd realized that she couldn't see him and wondered why he cared. He'd brought her to his mountain. Sooner or later he'd have to face her and explain what he wanted her to do. He hadn't expected to be drawn to the woman.

Twice before in his life he'd allowed himself to care about someone, and each time tragedy had occurred. Now his face was his punishment and his isolation his penance. The mountain was his sanctuary. He'd fostered the image and maintained the isolation, until he'd had no choice. If he were wise, he would keep his distance from the woman. For he knew the cost of allowing himself to care.

Still, for that one moment as their gazes melded in the moonlight, he'd felt a connection so intense that he tried to sever it. Then he'd remembered DeeDee's big eyes when he'd explained that Kaseybelle was coming for a visit. Bringing a smile to his daughter's face made anything bearable.

"Come on, Hap, let's go inside."

From woods beyond, a large dark gray and white Malamute appeared, dancing around Jonathan's feet. After giving a yelp of pleasure, he ran toward the castle, zigzagging back and forth as if he were connecting invisible dots to form a rope of tinsel on a Christmas tree.

Jonathan forced himself to relax his shoulders, then followed. He'd intended to see her that night, make all the arrangements, and put it behind him. But her plane had been late and he'd deliberately taken himself away from the house, alibiing his lack of courage by saying that he wanted to wait for DeeDee's reaction before he explained why he'd sent for Ms. Shannon Summers.

He stamped the snow from his feet and slipped inside the castle, listening. Satisfied that all was quiet, he went toward the kitchen in search of Mrs. Butterfield.

"She asked where you were, Mr. Jonathan."

"Did you deliver my message?"

"I did, but I just want you to know that I don't approve. This girl is not one of those—those floozies who used to follow after you. This is a sweet, nice girl, and she deserves to be treated properly. And don't go pretending that you're your own assistant like you do when you're doing business."

"John Drew doesn't have to explain his scars, Butter. Jonathan Dream would. As for Ms. Summers, any woman who is as successful as she is isn't likely to be a sweet, nice girl. Do you realize that singlehandedly from that little local three-person advertising agency she turned the Kissy Chocolate Company into a household world and helped create the hottest children's program on television?"

"Maybe, but I think she's nice, and it wouldn't do you any harm to remember that there are some old-fashioned girls left in the world. Just be honest with her."

"And let her know who Jonathan Dream is?"

"You're the same man you always were, Jonathan."

"No, I'm not, Butter. I'm not the same man at all. Did you show her the lingerie?"

"I told her it was there, but I don't think she'll wear any of it."

"And you'll be wrong. There isn't a woman in the world who'll turn down satin and lace if it's offered. Women are all alike in their secret minds."

"You'll see."

And two hours later he did.

The lights in the turret were still burning low. The woman was asleep. With hair like a splotch of spun gold against the pillow, she looked like some princess waiting to be kissed awake. He stood in the shadows, feeling vaguely uncomfortable, waiting for her to move, to lower the blanket so that he could see which of his NightDreams she'd chosen.

Over the years Jonathan Dream had done thorough research. The women who picked the burgundy satin and lace most often saw themselves as the subject of an old-world master painter. They were romantic and reserved. The white-silk wearers portrayed themselves as desirable and virginal. And then there were the women who wore black. They needed no cataloging. Their purpose and desires were universal.

He couldn't tell about Shannon Summers. She looked like a child, snuggled beneath the covers. For a moment he had the absurd thought that he'd like to be there with her, resting his head on her breasts, feeling that glorious hair tickle his face. The thought seemed to connect with a fine thread of heat that began to spin steadily downward until he felt the lurch between his legs. He shifted his position and willed the unwelcome thought away.

Women had been his inspiration, accounting for his monumental success and wealth. One had inspired a poor young boy to success beyond his wildest dreams and the other had caused him to turn away from it. Now a six-year-old child was forcing him to reach out again.

His guest let out a little sound and moved. The blanket slid down across one shoulder as she folded her arm behind her head, revealing a long-sleeved, pink flannel nightgown.

He hadn't expected that. He hadn't expected the continued strum of the connection between them as he watched pale, long lashes lie against a face as clear and innocent as a china doll's. And for a moment he forgot the pain in his life and his plan to avoid Shannon Summers. How could she be so appealing. He almost reached out to touch her cheek when he saw it beside her, the real doll, Kaseybelle, the chocolate company's fairy trademark, the reason he'd brought her here.

For Pete's sake, the woman was sleeping with a doll. No wonder she'd been so hard to deal with. She was probably some retarded genius who believed that the fairy was real. And he'd thought she would be good for DeeDee.

The absurdity of his sudden desire to touch her brought him soundly back to the present. Jonathan swung around and strode past the woman's bed and into the hall, pausing for one last moment to look back at Miss Shannon Summers, the woman who was going to bring a cartoon character to life for a little girl who couldn't walk.

Too bad she couldn't bring him to life as well. But his life had ended with the accident, with Mona, with DeeDee's legs, with the playboy persona he'd so carefully cultivated for so many years. Now Jonathan Dream was a legend, a phantom about whom fantasies and myths were created. And he was tired, very tired.

Unconsciously his fingertips sought the patch that covered his eye and part of the scar that crossed his cheekbone. The eye was gone, but the scar could be repaired. Only Jonathan knew that he'd refused plastic surgery, that this scar was his penance for the damage he'd done. The scar was on the surface, but the man beneath was just as flawed.

Two

Bright sunshine flooded the room, touching Shannon's face with points of light that gradually drew her awake. She stretched and curled beneath the blanket, waiting for memory to fully rouse her. She knew there was something intriguing beyond her closed eyelids. She'd even dreamed about him last night.

Him?

Jonathan Dream, the highwayman, the phantom of the snowcapped mountain. She dreamed that he'd stood in the shadows by her bed and stared down at her. He'd held out his hand as if he'd been asking something of her. And just for a second she'd wanted to tell him she understood. And then he'd gone.

Had she dreamed it? It had seemed so real.

It was impossible. No one could have stood by her bed. She'd locked her door, and she'd left the lights on. Shannon sat straight up. She studied the room and shook her head in disbelief. The lights were no longer burning. Who had turned out the lights? There had to be an explanation. And she intended to find it.

The shadowy figure she'd dreamed about was just that, a dream. She'd seen pictures of the extraordinarily handsome playboy who'd summoned her, and he didn't have long, flowing black hair. He was suave and sophisticated in his black shirts and silk suits. The man she'd studied before she'd come was nothing like the apparition who'd come to her in her dreams.

Willie, you're right. I do let my imagination run away with me. She'd promised to call him and let him know she'd arrived. He'd be worried about her.

Shannon took a quick shower, opened the bureau drawer to put away her gown, and caught sight of the sexy lace and satin inside. With a blush she slammed the drawer closed and stuffed her gown in her bag.

She braided her hair into a long plait that hung down her back, then thought better of how it looked and tied it with a black bow at the neck. Next she wound the braid around the bow, fastening it into a more professional style. Arriving with her hair flying loose the night before had been a mistake, but she'd been unable to relax on the plane with the rope of hair beneath her head and finally she'd loosened it, leaving it washboard curly for her arrival.

Changing only her blouse and underthings, she again dressed in the same black skirt and bolero jacket she'd worn on the plane. Then she pulled up the covers on the bed, placing Kaseybelle on top with her head on the pillow.

"You wait here, Kasey," she whispered, "while I try and get us out of here."

She intended to avoid the terrace, and the memory of the man standing on the cliff below, but in spite of her resolve she was pulled once more to the balcony. In the brilliant sunlight the centuries-old evergreens frosted white with snow were even more spectacular. Shannon felt as if she were standing on top of the world. As far as she could see, the mountains were swirls of white on green and laced with slivers of silvery granite winking in the sun.

Her eyes were drawn to the spot on the cliff.

She hadn't been dreaming. She could see that the snow had been disturbed where someone had stood. And there were animal prints, circling back toward the castle. Behind those prints were the human ones.

Shannon shivered, turned, and fled through the bedroom and down the circular stairs. Her imagination was both her most important asset and her biggest source of fear. With it she created, not only for the children of the world, but for herself as well. Sometimes the results gave her the secluded comfort she craved. Sometimes her thoughts were unwelcome.

Now she wanted coffee and a phone. Afterward she'd take on Jonathan Dream, and then she'd go home.

At least the coffee was within reach. Its smell drew her down the horseshoe staircase, through one of the arches, and toward the back of the house. Any pretense at reproducing the opera house in the living quarters ended with the large gray bricks and the shape of the structure. Downstairs the room reflected a much warmer, Moorish decor. Reds and golds blended with the gray.

Thick oriental carpets hugged marble floors, muffling her footsteps.

At the end of the corridor she stepped into a bright kitchen, where Mrs. Butter was filling a carafe that matched the one left by Shannon's bed. "Oh, you're up? I was just about to bring your breakfast."

"Mrs. Butterfield, you don't have to climb all those steps on my account. I'll just have coffee."

"Call me Butter, Shannon, and if you're sure, I'll just pour you a cup right here."

"That's fine. Then I'd like to meet with Mr. Drew as quickly as possible."

Mrs. Butterfield turned the cup around and around in her hands. "I'm sorry, but Mr. Jonathan was called away. He won't be able to see you until he returns tonight."

"Called away? But didn't he know I was here?"

"Yes, of course he did." In fact Mrs. Butterfield had chastised him for evading Shannon without an explanation and, worse, for being a coward.

Shannon groaned. "And he left? What am I supposed to do in the meantime?"

Mrs. Butterfield placed the cup on the table and pulled out a chair. "First, you eat." She poured the coffee and uncovered a plate of pastries on the tray. "Nothing feels right on an empty stomach."

Shannon sat down. It was a wonder she didn't weigh three hundred pounds. She'd heard that same line of reasoning for a good part of her childhood, every time her mother was about to leave again. As a child she'd thought of her mother as some beautiful fairy godmother swooping into her bedroom with her glittery cloak flying around her like a cloud. But there was no granting of wishes, nor bedtime stories for a lonely child.

There would be a quick kiss followed by an uncomfortable, "How is Mama's darling child? Are you doing your lessons and minding Nana?"

"Of course, Mommie," she'd answer as expected, always searching for a reason for her mother's unease, waiting for the hurting remark that would be sure to follow.

Sometimes it was, "Shannon, darling, I do wish you'd eat more. You're nothing but skin and bones." Other times it was, "Your hair. Tell Nana to find a way to restrain it. I just don't know where all those kinks came from," followed eventually by, "Well, never mind, love, we'll do something about it when you're older."

And then Mommie would be gone. Her imaginary companion Kaseybelle would appear along with Cook, who would bring chocolate and sweets and the promise that everything would be better on a full tummy. But it never was.

Shannon had filled out eventually, and one day she'd become too old to be her mother's child. So Mommie had become Sofia. Then Sofia had found that age became bearable only when she hid in alcohol and drugs.

Shannon had believed Sofia's agent when he'd said that her mother's death had been an accident. And then Shannon had been finally, truly alone.

Until Willie had come to the art institute looking for a student who would work cheap. Willie and the agency became the family she'd never had, and Kaseybelle, her imaginary companion throughout her childhood, had threatened to catapult Sofia Summers's shy daughter into the kind of world she'd always run away from.

"Mrs.—Butter, I left the lights on in my room

last night, and when I woke up this morning, they were off. I was sure I'd locked the door."

"All the locks can be operated electronically, Miss Summers. Mr. Jonathan had them installed that way so that DeeDee couldn't be . . . hurt."

"Hurt?"

"Well, you know how children are. He was afraid that she might venture up into one of the tower rooms and fall, or lock a door and not be able to get out."

"Then DeeDee is a child?"

"Of course. DeeDee is six years old. Didn't he tell you?"

"He's told me nothing, except that he's interested in my taking on a temporary assignment on behalf of Expressions."

"What's Expressions?"

Shannon added milk and sweetener to her coffee and sipped it. Of course there was no reason to believe that a housekeeper would know anything about advertising, be a part of whatever scheme Jonathan Dream was formulating. But she seemed to be more than a servant.

"The agency I work for."

"But I thought that you were Kaseybelle."

"Well, I am—at least Kaseybelle is my creation. I made her the logo for Kissy Chocolates. Now she's a cartoon character—"

"Gracious, you don't have to explain. I know who Kaseybelle is. I haven't heard anything else but Kaseybelle for three months. Mr. Jonathan says that if anyone can get DeeDee up and going, it's Kaseybelle. I'm truly glad you've come. DeeDee needs you."

Mrs. Butterfield refilled Shannon's cup and motioned for her to bring the platter of pastries. "Come along, I'll take you to her."

"But I—I think I'd better wait for Mr. Drew. And I need to call my office."

"Later. Now you should come with me."

Shannon had no choice but to comply. Redirecting Mrs. Butterfield was akin to capturing spilled milk. She went everywhere at once. Mrs. Butter led her down the corridor she'd traveled earlier, to a door that opened into an enormous room that was all windows. There were green trees, flowers, even a small indoor pool, large enough for a child.

"A solarium," Shannon said softly. "How lovely."

The flowers and the blooming trees seemed incongruous with the snow and ice beyond, but nothing seemed as out of place as the small figure in the wheelchair. She was as still as a cat, poised for attack, but the life had gone out of her, allowing her small head to lean listlessly against the chair back. In front of her was a table, laid with breakfast things.

"Look, DeeDee, you have a guest for breakfast."

"Don't want a guest."

"But you don't even know who it is."

"Doesn't matter."

"Try to reach her, Shannon," Mrs. Butterfield whispered under her breath. "Mr. Jonathan is certain that Kaseybelle can perform miracles."

"Kaseybelle?" Was that why she'd been practically kidnapped? Because a six-year-old in a wheelchair needed cheering up?

"Kaseybelle?" The little girl repeated, sat up, and turned her head. A glimmer of surprise flashed across her face. "You're not my th'rpist?"

"No, I'm an artist." Shannon found herself walking toward the child. Venting her anger on

Jonathan Drew was one thing, but a handicapped child didn't deserve her censure.

The man standing on the loft above the solarium waited with half-held breath. The woman was taller than he'd thought. Her hair was as golden in the sunlight as it had been last night on her pillow, and she was just as appealing. He hadn't expected that.

There was something truly innocent about her. And he found himself watching her graceful movements, the way her eyes lit up, the curve of her lips as she smiled. She brought sunshine into the room and—he searched his mind for the emotion, then gave it a name—the promise of joy.

He watched, noting the flush of color on her cheeks and the way her lace blouse caressed her neck under her chin and peaked out from beneath the tailored jacket. There was something intriguing about the tailored exterior and the feminine softness hidden beneath that hardness.

His daughter's voice caught him and forced his attention to his plan. "You draw pictures?" she asked.

"Yes. I draw pictures that are sometimes made into cartoons. Do you know what a cartoon is?"

"Of course I do. I may be sick, but I can read and play all the electronic games. And watch television. My daddy bought a special dish antenna so that I can watch hundreds of channels. My daddy buys me anything I want."

"And what do you want, DeeDee?" Shannon asked, sliding into a chair Mrs. Butterfield had placed on the other side of the child's breakfast table.

"I want—It doesn't matter what I want," she

said, losing the flash of animation in her voice and leaning back in her chair. "Daddy can't buy it."

"Well, I don't know. He's bought you fairy food."

"Fairy food?" Her eyes brightened, then narrowed in disbelief. "You know about fairy food?"

"I have a very good friend who knows everything about fairy food."

"You do? Who?"

"I first met her when I was about your age. Her name is Kaseybelle."

"You know Kaseybelle? You really, truly know Kaseybelle?"

"I really, truly know Kaseybelle."

And then Jonathan knew he'd done the right thing by blackmailing Shannon Summers into coming to his secret place.

With the mention of that one word, Kaseybelle, he saw the wonder return to his daughter's eyes, the joy that had once brought laughter to the castle and warmth to his heart. And it all came from an imaginary character who'd become the logo for a candy company, Kaseybelle, the Kissy Chocolate fairy.

It was mid-afternoon and Shannon was still in her traveling clothes. She was beginning to feel grungy and more than a little angry.

DeeDee had been put down for a nap. An ordinary six-year-old would have been insulted by the proposition, but after a morning of stories, followed by a painful session with her live-in therapist and a lunch that changed from soup and crackers to Kaseybelle's special elixir and pixie puffs, DeeDee was worn out.

Shannon felt a shiver of anxiety skate down her

spine. All morning she'd felt as if someone were watching her.

Watching. The man on the cliff had been watching. There'd been that same kind of eerie awareness when he'd turned to look up at her. Then later, in her dream, she'd felt the connection snap into place. Her shiver wasn't one of cold or fear, it was more an intuition, an anticipation that was quite unlike anything she'd ever experienced. And it made her anxious.

A walk. She could work off some of her tension with a walk through the woods. The cliff beneath her window beckoned to her. Leaving her room, she went in search of Mrs. Butterfield, who was again in the kitchen.

"Mrs. Butter, I wonder if I might borrow a heavy coat. I'd like to take a walk, but when I left Atlanta, I didn't anticipate weather like this."

"Certainly. There's a clothes rack by the back door. Just pick whatever you want. You'll need gloves and a head covering too."

Shannon followed her directions and found a heavy black cape. She fastened it over her shoulders, thrust a pair of furry white gloves in her pocket, and pulled a white fur hat on her head.

Outside the door the scene could have been a snow-covered wood in old Russia. It's this place, she told herself, it's enough to make you think about mystery and illusion. She threaded her fingers into the gloves and started walking toward the tree line. The snow was deeper than she'd expected, and her boots were more decorative than practical. But still she continued, the shivery feeling following her like an unseen companion.

Jonathan's study filled the lower floor of the turret. From the window he watched her planting her feet in the footprints he'd made the night before. She didn't go any farther than the clearing.

She turned slowly around, studying the castle and the woods. In spite of the seriousness of her examination he decided that she looked like a child who saw gingerbread houses instead of castles made of stone. Her lips were pressed together in suppressed delight. And she was very beautiful, a vision of black and white and gold against the snow.

Then she dropped to her knees on the ground. A moment later Hap came bounding from the woods and into her open arms. He greeted her as if she were a long-lost friend, planting his big paws against her, knocking her back in the snow. She let out a little cry of alarm. Fearfully Jonathan came to his feet, intent on calling off the dog, who might not be as friendly as he appeared.

At that moment the woman's gaze moved to the window, and Jonathan stepped back. He didn't think she could see him, but he was supposed to be away for the day. Being caught in a deliberate lie would make his proposition difficult. But more than that, he felt shame. From what he'd learned about his guest, she'd been the victim of years of emotional blackmail by her mother and now he was subjecting her to more subterfuge. He was sorry, but he couldn't worry about the woman or acknowledge his concern for her. It was DeeDee who was important.

From below she felt his presence. There was only a flicker of movement and the shadowy suggestion of someone watching from the window. But he was there. And it came to her that she'd felt him watching her for most of the day. The sensation wasn't threatening, rather it was of curiosity. Nevertheless she'd had enough mystery.

"Relax, Shan," Willie had said earlier when she'd finally reached him. "Dream's assistant, Lawrence, called last night and let me know that you arrived safely."

"Oh, they had time for you but not for me. I think that Jonathan Dream is a rude, overbearing man."

"Now, now, Shan. Most women would envy you, on top of a mountain with Jonathan Dream. What more could you want?"

"An interview, an apology, a little courtesy, and a return ticket, in that order."

It was the interview that was most on her mind. She'd had enough of shadows and conflicting emotions. One minute she felt his presence so acutely that she expected him to speak, the next minute an aura of childish curiosity seemed to settle over her.

"Ah, Shan," Willie was saying, "take it easy. I know you aren't interested in wealth and fame, but I am. Our new building is almost finished, and Expressions is ready to cross the threshold of greatness. All we need is the NightDreams sleepwear account. It's important, Shan. If this works out, I'll even make you a partner."

"I don't want to be a partner, Willie. I like our arrangement just as it is. At least I have until now."

"Isn't there something I can do to make you see this through? Shan, it's time you broke out of your ivory tower and let the world see the real you. Don't you have any secret dreams?"

"No!" At least she hadn't until she'd arrived there. "What I'd like you to do is—is—make Mr.

Dream get out of my dreams. If there's a lake in the basement of this place, Willie, I'm out of here."

"He hasn't—I mean he didn't—"

Willie might be a free spirit, but Shannon knew how protective he was of her. He'd understood her need for privacy and had been her shield against the world. She didn't want to give him the wrong impression. Jonathan Dream might be secretive, but he'd done nothing to compromise her.

"Don't worry, Willie." She started to say she hadn't seen him, then remembered the man in the snow and changed her statement to, "I don't think I've laid eyes on the man yet, unless you count the nightmare I had last evening. This place is spooky."

"Any new place is spooky to you, Shannon. I know this is hard for you, but try to relax and enjoy your visit."

But she couldn't relax. Even the big dog, with his joyous welcome, didn't erase the feeling of unease. Now she was seeing shadows in windows and feeling things that she couldn't understand.

The snow was wet and cold, and she'd been out in it long enough. She'd go back inside and take a nap. Mr. Dream was due to return by dinnertime, and she'd finally complete her mission.

With the dog loping along beside her, she made her way back to the house. Returning the clothing to the rack, she allowed her fingertips to brush the thick jacket on the last hook. There was a curious tingle when she touched it, as though it was surrounded by an energy field.

The man last night had been wearing a thick jacket.

The man who had to have been Jonathan Dream.

The man who was a phantom.

• • •

Jonathan Dream didn't return in time for dinner. Shannon had finally given up and gone to bed, only to be wakened by Mrs. Butterfield.

"Mr. Dream will see you now," she said. "Wear this and come with me." She handed Shannon a velvet dressing gown, nothing like the sheer clothing in the bureau. Shannon hesitated for a moment, then, deciding that getting the meeting behind her was more important than how she looked, she slid her arms into the long fitted sleeves, buttoned the front to the waist, and slipped her feet into the matching velvet shoes.

Now Shannon was pacing back and forth in the study, growing more alarmed by the moment. If Mr. Dream didn't appear soon, she was out of there, even if she had to tie her sheets together and go over the wall.

There was a crackling fire in the massive fireplace and music playing softly on a stereo. But the room was empty. Butter had backed away quickly, closing the door behind her without explanation.

Flickering firelight created more shadows falling across the chairs and the sofa near the fire. In the darkest end of the room was an enormous desk and a chair that was turned toward the two windows, now framing the moonlit winter night.

The grandfather clock began to chime.

Midnight.

"Have a seat, Ms. Summers."

Shannon started. She'd believed the room was empty. It wasn't. There was someone in the chair.

"Mr. Dream, it is Mr. Dream, isn't it?"

"I am Jonathan Dream, yes."

"I don't understand why you brought me here. I know nothing about hard-sell advertising campaigns, or costs, or proposals."

"I don't care about advertising campaigns, Ms. Summers. Your Willie can handle that. I brought you here for my daughter, to bring her back to life."

Shannon let out a shocked cry of disbelief. "You did what?"

"I know you spent the afternoon with DeeDee. You know she's in a wheelchair. The doctor thought that after the last operation, with work and braces, she could walk again. But the therapy is painful, and she's been through so much. She isn't cooperating with her therapist. She'd given up—until I promised her that Kaseybelle would come to help her."

"You didn't."

"I did. I'd do almost anything to make my daughter happy, including buying an imaginary fairy, if that's what it takes."

"Kaseybelle isn't for sale."

"Maybe not, but there's you. How much do you cost, Ms. Summers? I'm buying." He didn't know why he was being so severe, unless it was his unexpected attraction to the woman. He needed to reinforce his authority. Or did he? He stared at her as he considered what he was feeling.

He was going too fast. She was hearing his words, but she was having trouble with their meaning. People weren't for sale, at least not her. She lost his voice for a moment, then caught it again as he said something about a contract, not for advertising, but for . . . her services?

Shannon could understand the man's phenomenal success. With a voice that wrapped around her, he was very persuasive. And for one incredible moment she wanted to agree—to whatever he was asking of her. She shook her head, trying to break the invisible link he had forged between them. She didn't want to care about him.

"Turn around, Mr. Dream. I'm not for sale, and even if I were, I won't do business with a man who isn't willing to deal with me face-to-face."

"But I was told that you conduct all your work by telephone and computer. Even your employer thought you would understand my unique situation and need for privacy. I can offer you anything you want."

"I don't want anything, except to keep my life from changing."

"But that isn't possible, is it?"

For a moment she looked frightened, and he understood. There'd been a time when he felt that way, before he'd realized what was happening to DeeDee—and to himself. "Please hear me out."

"All right," she agreed. She ought to insist that he let her leave immediately, but she didn't. Once more that curious connection held her, along with the suggestion of a vulnerability that was as strong as her own. In spite of his thorny exterior, he couldn't quite mask the truth. There was something about this man's need to hide his inner goodness under the guise of being a bitter recluse that made her listen.

"I'm not what people think," he finally said.

"None of us are. We all hide in different ways. Why didn't you meet my plane?"

"I never go into Asheville!"

"No? You only go into locked bedrooms and watch people while they sleep. Was I what you expected?"

"No, but I didn't expect anything. You saw me?"

"I wasn't certain I had—until now. Turn around, Mr. Dream. Please. Whatever the problem is, I'll understand."

"Perhaps you will."

The chair began to swivel. At that moment the already-dim lights went out, leaving only the flickering fire, which washed the room with a warm glow.

Shannon forgot her fear and took a step closer. All she could see was an outline, a dark image of a man that blended in with the oversize chair in which he was sitting.

"Turn on the light," she said softly.

"No. A night dream never survives the light."

"Why? Are you afraid of me?"

He was tempted to rise, walk over to her, and challenge her statement. He wanted to reach out and touch her hair, feel the hesitancy of her breathing against his cheek. The wanting kept coming at him from out of nowhere. He couldn't allow that to happen. That wasn't part of the plan.

"Maybe I am afraid. Sit down, Shannon. We'll talk."

She came closer, sitting in the chair opposite the desk. As her eyes became more accustomed to the darkness, she began to distinguish the features on the man who was sitting half-turned to her, his face a profile in the flickering shadows.

"That's better. You get on well with my daughter. I'm pleased."

"You were watching?"

"Yes."

His honesty surprised her. "I knew. I felt you."

That surprised him. He'd thought he was the

only one caught up in the connection between them.

"Why did you have Mrs. Butterfield lie about your being away?"

"I'm sorry," he admitted. He owed her that. "I wanted to observe you with DeeDee. If the meeting had been a failure, I would have let you go immediately."

"What about Willie and the NightDream advertising account?"

"Oh, that. I spoke with Willie this morning. You can have the account so long as I get what I want. And I've already told you, Ms. Summers. I want you."

"Mr. Dream, you could probably have anyone you want, why me? I'm not your kind of woman. I'm not good with people. I don't mix easily and I'm not very brave. The truth is, I know nothing about handling children."

"You're wrong. Only a very special person could create a character who touches children the way yours does." He didn't want to think about how she'd already touched him.

"I don't understand."

"Let me try to explain. My daughter wants Kaseybelle, the Chocolate Fairy. And I expect—no, I'm asking you to give her what she wants."

"How?"

"Draw her pictures. Tell her stories. Watch the program with her, whatever it takes to get her out of that damned chair."

"But, Mr. Dream—"

"Please, call me Jonathan."

She couldn't. That made it personal. "The Kaseybelle character belongs to the candy company and their television studio now. I don't own her anymore."

"I know, but DeeDee doesn't know that."

"I like DeeDee, Mr.—Jonathan—and I'm so sorry about her problem, but I can't give her what I don't have. Now, I'd like to go back to Atlanta. I'd planned to leave this morning."

Jonathan hated what he was doing. But he expected her to agree because she cared about Willie. He liked Shannon and he approved of her loyalty. That was real. He stood and walked to the window.

"For every day you stay with my daughter, your firm gets my advertising for one year. I'll set up an office here so that you can work, and you can name your own price."

"I can't. I really can't."

His fist crashed against the wall by the window. Then he leaned his head against his arm. "Ms. Summers, there are ways to force people to do almost anything. I'd rather not do this, but I must. If you don't agree to my terms, I'll buy the candy company and destroy Kaseybelle and your friend Willie Hicks as well."

"You wouldn't dare."

"I don't want to, but I would." There was no mistaking his determination, nor his attempt to control his desperation. Finally, from somewhere in that terrible state of his despair, he said, "Do you want me to beg? Fine, I will. Please!"

She could have lived with his anger, but not his pain. And she couldn't let others be hurt because of her. Whatever the world said about him, he had great capacity for love. She wondered what it would feel like to be the recipient of that kind of powerful emotion.

"Don't beg, Jonathan. You don't understand. It isn't that you haven't offered enough. It's me. I simply can't do what you ask. I'd be afraid."

"Afraid? You don't know what it is to fear. To watch someone you love shrivel up inside, to feel the most important thing in your life die."

Whatever other lies he'd perpetrated, Jonathan Dream was telling the truth now. His request wasn't for himself. He was in deep pain, and she could feel the darkness that threatened to engulf him. But he was wrong. The pain didn't touch only DeeDee. It was his. It was more.

"What happened to DeeDee?"

"There was a wreck. The car sailed off the mountain. She was left a cripple."

"And her mother? What happened to her?"

He turned from the window, turned and took a step toward her.

"Her mother? Her mother's dead."

"How?"

"How? I killed her."

A log broke and the flame flared.

The man standing before her squared his shoulders and lifted his face to the firelight. The man she'd seen in the snow. The man she'd seen standing over her bed. The phantom she'd dreamed about. He had a horrible scar across his face and a patch over one eye.

Three

She must have slept the second night, but she couldn't be sure. Her dreams were filled with the face of the man wearing a patch over his left eye. She heard his stern voice, snatches of phrases, words that made her feel afraid yet strangely drawn to him.

Did he ever smile or let himself feel joy? As isolated as she'd always been, she'd found simple pleasures rewarding. But she didn't think that Jonathan Dream ever relaxed.

The next morning she was very tired, her mind was fraught with tension. She didn't believe for a minute that he'd killed his wife. Any man who cared enough about a child to buy a fairy to make the child happy couldn't have hurt anybody. He was only warning her, telling her to stay away. Still, there was something dark about the man.

Shannon dragged herself from bed, trying to separate how she wished things to be from how they were. The truth was, she couldn't be certain that any decision she made would be rational.

Somehow she'd been bewitched, and the only safe thing for her to do was leave.

Dress first, she decided, then call a cab and have it meet her at the gate. That way she'd be gone before anyone knew—before she fell under the spell of the castle's magic—before she acknowledged the power of the man who'd brought her here. Yes. That's what she'd do.

Now that she'd made her decision, she was impatient to be gone. She went to the closet—

Her traveling suit was gone. Hanging in its place were . . . fairy clothes? She stared in disbelief. The prototype costumes she'd had made up as samples of Kaseybelle's wardrobe were hanging in her closet. How?

Jonathan Dream. He'd done this. He hadn't waited for her decision. It was as if he'd known what she planned and had circumvented her actions before she could carry them out. Even if he was one of the wealthiest, most powerful men in the world, she'd dealt with power and wealth all her life. She might not have been able to stand up to her mother, but this man was about to learn that she could fling a full-fledged, mouth-full-of-nails temper tantrum.

But not in her nightgown. If the only way she could get to Mr. Dream was as a fairy, that's what she'd be. She pulled on a pair of lavender leotards, the matching filmy jacket constructed of what looked like spun silk, and the golden slippers that Kaseybelle always wore. She pulled a brush through her hair and dashed downstairs.

She could hear DeeDee's voice and the murmur of Mrs. Butterfield's bright, ongoing monologue. First Shannon intended to talk to Jonathan Dream. She headed for the study.

Empty. At least the room was empty of any physical presence. Still, it swirled with the rush of emotion that seemed to permeate the very air. The phone. She might as well call for her cab while she had the opportunity. There was no telephone directory. Let Mr. Dream pay for the information call, she thought, he owed her. She lifted the receiver. There was no dial tone. Impatiently she jiggled the buttons. Nothing.

Either the phone was out of order or the system was another one of those things that were controlled electronically by Jonathan Dream. Shannon's head ached. She was getting very tired of the melodrama.

She whirled around and headed for the kitchen. Mrs. Butterfield could tell her where Jonathan was. She'd demand to know. She'd—

"Kaseybelle!" DeeDee stopped the glass she was about to drink from in mid-air and let out a wondrous sigh of contentment. "I knew all along that you were really Kaseybelle. My daddy was right. You're so beautiful."

"My, my." Even Mrs. Butterfield was awestruck. "You're the spitting image of that fairy, all right. No wonder your hair startled me so when you got here yesterday."

Shannon pressed her lips together and stepped into the room. This entire incident had gone too far. She had a great deal of respect for a father who cared enough for his child to make her happy. But happiness couldn't be bought.

She was living proof of that. Her mother had tried and failed. Shannon had learned early that happiness had to come from inner strength, and depending on a fairy to provide it was an illusion.

Sure, but isn't that what you did? a little voice

inside her head asked, a voice she ignored, at least to begin with.

"Nonsense, DeeDee, I'm not Kaseybelle. This is just one of her costumes. You remember that I told you I draw her. I always have her fairy clothes made up so that I can see the garments I've visualized."

"Oh, yes, Kasey," DeeDee said with delight, oblivious to the point that Shannon was trying to make. "Come and eat. Mrs. Butter has made more elixir and fairy puffs."

"Mrs. Butterfield, where is Mr. Dream?"

"I believe he's in your office, Shannon."

"*My* office? *My* office is in Atlanta, on Peachtree Street, between Thirteenth and Fourteenth Streets, on the second floor of a building that used to house a flower shop. The window boxes are still there."

"And Kaseybelle grows geraniums in the window boxes, I know," DeeDee added. "I saw them on her program."

Shannon couldn't seem to stop the tide that was sweeping her along with its force. "All right, Mrs. Butter, where is *my* office?"

"Past Mr. Jonathan's office, second door on the right."

She should have expected what she found, but she didn't. Nobody had the power to act that quickly. He'd duplicated her office exactly. Her desk, her drawing table, her books and supplies, just as they'd been left in Atlanta, were all there. And Jonathan Dream was sitting behind her desk as if he'd been waiting.

"If there's anything else you need, just tell me and it'll be here in a matter of hours."

"What I need, Mr. Dream, are answers."

"Ask the questions."

"I've seen pictures of you and they don't show either a scar or an eye patch. Are you really Jonathan Dream?"

"I am. I lost my eye and gained the scar in the same accident that killed my wife three years ago."

"I see, and you've managed to keep all that a secret from the world? I don't think so."

"If you have enough money, you can do almost anything. This castle gave me the idea. When I need to meet with the outside world, I do so as John, my assistant. No one knows that the scarred man is Jonathan Dream except Mrs. Butterfield and Lawrence. And now you."

"I would never betray a confidence. I promise to keep yours, in exchange for your honesty."

"Agreed."

"About your wife," Shannon persisted. "You didn't kill her. A man who cares so much about a child couldn't kill anyone."

"Not with my hands, but I was responsible for the accident. As far as I'm concerned, that's enough proof of guilt."

"That's fantasy. What I need is reality and control."

"Why?"

"Because this is my life, and I'll make the decisions about what I do with it."

"Once I thought that was possible. I know now that we have very little control over what happens to us. Fantasy makes as much sense as anything else."

"But I'm not a fairy. That's wrong. You've made your daughter believe that I'm Kaseybelle, and I'm not."

"No?"

In profile she would see a hesitant smile play about the corner of his lips, a smile she was certain he wasn't aware of. And that smile subtly altered the darkness around him. She felt an absurd urge to smile in return, an urge that she forcibly swallowed.

Jonathan watched her change of expression play across her face. He had known how appealing she was from a distance. He hadn't expected to feel such fire when they met face-to-face. He'd always been a man of few words, now even those escaped him.

Not Kaseybelle? Could she not know what she'd done? Perhaps she'd never seen herself dressed like this. Perhaps he, too, was bemused and seeing only what he wanted to see. She didn't look real. No matter what she said, Shannon Summers was a spirit, a creature from some make-believe world that existed in the imagination or in a dream.

It was time she learned some reality.

Jonathan didn't realize he'd moved until he was standing beside her. "Take my hand, Shannon, and turn around."

"No!"

He held out his hand. "Yes."

She allowed him to direct her movement so that they were facing a mirror hanging above the fireplace. In the moonlight he'd been hidden. In the shadows of his office his face hadn't been exposed until he'd come into the firelight. Now he was inviting her to look.

His long hair flowed across the top of his shoulders in a rippling black mass. Like the highwayman she'd compared him to, he was wearing a black shirt, open at the neck, and black trousers and polished black boots.

But it was his face she saw, the face he apparently wanted her to see, and the black satin patch that covered his left eye. The patch didn't conceal the disfiguring scar that ran from his eyebrow to the top of his cheek.

He simply glared at her, waiting.

"I'm not afraid of your face, Jonathan Dream. You don't have to hide in the darkness on my account. Your face neither intimidates me nor frightens me. I don't judge a person by his looks. It's what's inside that counts."

"Looks count, too, sometimes. Face the mirror, Shannon, and you'll see what I mean."

She forced her gaze from the man in black in the mirror to the woman beside him. No, not the woman, the spirit in the familiar fairy clothing.

She gasped. Why had she never before understood? Kaseybelle, the fairy she'd lovingly brought to life as the embodiment of love and caring, was her, not as she was now but as she had been as a little girl. She'd created a friend for a lonely child, and the only model she'd had was herself.

"You see what DeeDee sees and what she needs?"

"No, I won't have it," Shannon whispered raggedly. "I'm real. I have needs too. What about what I need?"

"Just say what it is and I'll get it."

To be loved, is what she wanted to say, *intensely*. By a *man who feels as passionately as I do.* "My freedom," was her desperate answer.

He felt the muscles of his stomach contract. "Anything but that. I can't let you leave. But if you stay here, I may destroy you. Everything I touch is left tarnished."

He was still holding her arm, clasping her in such a way that he could feel her pulse thrumming beneath his fingertips. Or was it his? Even in the mirror he could see her apprehension. Like some night creature frozen in the light, she seemed ready to flee, yet unable to move. Her lips parted, and her breath, fast and shallow, barely moved her lungs.

"Shannon, don't be afraid," he said, and knew that he couldn't let her go. "Give DeeDee one month, until Christmas, and if you still want to go, I won't object."

He was asking, not demanding, and she knew she couldn't refuse.

"Why do I feel like Scheherazade?" she finally asked.

His eyebrows were question marks. "Who?"

"Have you never read *The Arabian Nights*?"

"No, I don't think so."

"There was an ancient Persian king who discovered his wife plotting against him. He killed her. In order to prevent any woman from deceiving him again, he married a wife in the morning and killed her the next morning. Then Scheherazade came along. She conceived the idea of telling a story on the morning before her execution. She so captured the king's fancy with her tales that each morning he let her live another night."

"Do you think you can capture my fancy?" The suggestion of a half-smile spread across his lips, and he let out a genuine laugh that surprised them both.

"Oh, no. But, like Scheherazade, I must remain

here and please you by telling stories to your daughter, whether or not I wish to stay."

Now she was smiling, too, and in the mirror he could see the visible altering of the tension between them. "Yes. I suppose that's true. I'm sorry it must be that way. I wish you'd stay willingly, because you choose to."

He turned her away from the mirror so that she was gazing at his face, so that he could be certain her fear was gone. And what he saw in the mirror behind was a reflection of himself, glaring at her with all the heat of the coals in the fire the night before.

She started to speak, but the connection between them intensified and the power of his presence immobilized her, took her words away. "Mr.—"

He cut her off. "Don't make me into something I'm not, Shannon. You're right to be afraid of me. I always hurt the ones I care about. And no matter how impossible it may be, I think I could care for you."

"No, please don't. You mustn't. Let me go."

"I can't." He inclined his head, bringing his lips closer. His grip changed from desperation to a plea. With a soft caressing touch, he drew her hand to his chest and felt her fingertips slip beneath the shirt, where they found bare, hot skin.

"Jonathan?"

She didn't know whether she was asking him to release her or to carry her farther into the sea of emotional intensity he'd created. What she was feeling was all new to her, new and powerful and frightening.

He was so very tall and strong and foreboding.

Desire, wild and hypnotic, rushed through Shannon, even as she realized the danger. Part of her wanted to push him away, while another part wanted to stand on tiptoe to reach him.

"Will you, Ms. Summers?" He brushed her lips with his own lightly, leaving a trail of heat like powdery sugar on a hot fried doughnut.

"Will I what?"

"Stay with us? Help my daughter?"

"Yes." She heard her answer, the soft, uncertain yes, so unexpected and so strange that her answer could have come from someone else.

"Thank you!" Jonathan heard his voice turn hoarse. His control was dangerously near being broken. His head felt light. What in hell was happening? Almost angrily he dropped her hands and stepped away, staring at her as if he'd been sleepwalking and suddenly awakened.

"I'll have suitable clothing provided, and your phone will be connected. Whatever you need is yours. I'll leave you now."

And he was gone.

Shannon shook her head, trying to throw off the sense of unreality that had swept over her. What had she done? How had he managed to get her to agree to his demand? He'd captured her with his voice, his words, his pain. She still couldn't believe the sequence of events that had transpired over the last forty-eight hours.

Twice in her life she'd faced the unrelenting power of another person's control and failed to conquer it. The first adversary had been her mother. Now she'd succumbed to the magnetism of Jonathan Dream.

But there was one difference. Her mother had dominated her under the guise of motherly love and the constant demand for unending adoration from her child in return. Jonathan wasn't asking for anything for himself, but for DeeDee. And he used the threat that he'd buy the chocolate company to force Shannon to accede to his wishes. He couldn't know that his real control came from the power of his own magnetism. She could only hope that he didn't understand how deeply she'd been affected.

Shannon collapsed into the chair behind her desk and rested her face on her arms. She'd never found a way to escape her mother's dominance; she couldn't let that happen again. She'd stay for a month. She'd spend every moment with DeeDee. Once she'd accomplished her assignment, he'd be forced to let her go. In the meantime she'd find a way to avoid Jonathan Dream.

With the back of her hand she rubbed her lips.

The friction only increased the warmth. And her fingertips continued to tingle.

Four

DeeDee's tutor had come and gone for the day. From the loft above the sun room Jonathan watched his daughter having her legs manipulated by her therapist. Music was playing, happy music spilling across the room like the calliope from a traveling circus. Instead of tears there was laughter.

Because of Kaseybelle the Chocolate Fairy.

Because of Shannon Summers.

The first thing Shannon had done was to move the therapy equipment into the solarium so that DeeDee didn't feel so intimidated by the sterile atmosphere. Jonathan didn't know why he hadn't thought of that. The mood changed even more when the therapist, an energetic young woman who lived in the castle, was persuaded to don one of the fairy costumes and turn the exercises into part of a story that Shannon composed during their sessions.

Jonathan had tried to stay away. Always before, the pain DeeDee had endured had so unnerved him that he couldn't bear to watch. It was his fault, and every tear she'd shed fell like ice on his emotions. He wished he could endure it for her, then cursed because he could not. For so long she'd been so brave, and so alone.

He was alone, too, but that and the scarred face was all he deserved. He'd forfeited any chance at more long ago when he'd surrounded himself by people who were dishonest. And it had been Mona, beautiful and innocent, who'd traveled down a long white corridor sweetened with a different kind of snow.

Jonathan had never needed anything but his own energy to get high. But without his knowledge he'd been the provider. He could have claimed ignorance of what his money had done to the young women who'd hungered for fame, but he didn't. He should have known about the secret drugs being funneled into his Dreamland estate, but he'd been so caught up in building a dynasty that he'd been blind to what was happening.

Until Mona had announced her pregnancy . . . until he'd learned that in spite of his attempts to maintain his emotional distance from those he kept around him, he'd fathered a child . . . until he'd learned that Mona was taking drugs. He'd done the only right thing: He'd married her.

Mona had expected the good times to continue, the bright lights and fame to be enhanced. She'd never expected him to change everything. But he'd completed the castle on top of the North Carolina mountain and moved them there. He'd quickly learned that isolation was the only way of making certain that Mona took care of herself, that his baby had a chance.

But Mona hadn't been able to change. If he'd

really loved her, everything might have been different, but he'd only been able to love her as the mother of his child. That hadn't been enough.

And in the end he, too, had died. Until now, watching his daughter smile and laugh, work at the exercises to strengthen muscles and tendons, work toward reaching a goal that as yet lay unstated, he'd thought that his life was over. Now, like DeeDee, he felt the stirring of something he couldn't allow himself to name.

Jonathan had intended to stay away from the loft, but he couldn't. At first Shannon had fought against his demands that she stay. His threat to destroy Kaseybelle, the thing she loved most, hadn't entirely worked. Not until he'd pleaded with her to stay had she agreed. Not until he'd laughed out loud. Then, once she'd agreed to help, she'd thrown herself into the program with such enthusiasm that he'd been drawn to the solarium to watch.

Looking like little more than a child herself, she seemed to understand and share DeeDee's anxieties and find a way to soothe her concerns. Though Jonathan had arranged for other clothing, she'd continued to wear the soft gold-and-pastel-colored fairy costumes around DeeDee.

"It hurts, Kaseybelle. Why do I have to do it?"

"We often have to do things we don't want to. Look at that squirrel, running about digging in the snow. He had to spend all summer and fall burying nuts instead of playing squirrel games. I'm sure his hands were very sore from digging."

"Squirrels have hands?"

"Certainly they do. How else could they have tea parties if they couldn't hold the acorn shells?"

"Squirrels have tea parties? I don't believe it."

"Well, they aren't really tea parties. They take the nuts and boil them. Then they drink their juice from little acorn hulls."

"Ah, you're telling me fairy stories now, Kaseybelle. Where do they get the fire?"

"They borrow it from the sun. But they have to be very careful. If they take too much sunshine, it will burn the nuts up and start a forest fire."

"My daddy wouldn't let them start a fire around here. He works very hard and he's very careful."

"Of course he is, and so are the squirrels."

"But my daddy doesn't have sore hands like the squirrels."

"No."

"But his face hurts," DeeDee said softly. "I know because when he doesn't know I'm looking, sometimes he rubs it. Do you think that you could help my daddy fix his face?"

Jonathan winced. He hadn't been aware that he touched his face. It was an involuntary gesture, not from pain but to remind him that his world was under control. He leaned forward, interested in Kaseybelle's reply.

"I don't know, DeeDee. Sometimes there are things that we can't fix."

"But you could use your fairy magic. I know you could."

"Perhaps your daddy doesn't want anything to change."

DeeDee thought about that for a moment. "Yes, he does. He wants me to walk. That's why my legs have to hurt."

From above, Jonathan acknowledged the wisdom of his daughter's words. She was right. That's why people suffered pain, to change. But sometimes the change hurt others and that's when the pain became a constant reminder of guilt.

Jonathan found it hard to concentrate on the business of running NightDreams Lingerie. He knew that during DeeDee's school time Shannon dealt with her world of chocolate and cartoons from the office he'd provided for her use. He didn't intrude, using the time to run his manufacturing plants, his chain of retail stores, and his catalog business. But he'd find himself, at the oddest moments, thinking of flannel nightgowns instead of slinky teddies and flowing negligees.

And he couldn't seem to stay away from the solarium.

Today Shannon had surprised him by doing something he'd never done, donning one of the swimsuits he'd provided and going into the pool with DeeDee. He didn't know why *he'd* never been in the indoor pool he'd had built.

Moments later he was walking through the solarium in a swimsuit. When DeeDee looked up and saw him, it made his decision worthwhile. When Shannon smiled in approval, it didn't matter whether her approval was because of DeeDee or because she welcomed the visit.

They'd held on and kicked like whales for nearly half an hour. Mrs. Butter had fetched DeeDee and left Jonathan and Shannon sitting on the side of the pool, watching a light snow fall across the trees in the late-afternoon light.

"How'd you find your castle?"

"By accident. I wanted something special as far away from my past life as I could find. Lawrence found this place. The original builder had started the castle, then fell into bankruptcy, leaving it half done. The facsimile to the Paris Opera House caught my fancy."

Jonathan's body was lean and firm. She was reminded of some sleek jungle animal, a panther perhaps, always tightly wound and ready to spring. Yet this afternoon he seemed to relax. The aura of mystery was there, yet it was no longer ominous.

"How long have you been here?"

"We came before DeeDee was born. It was a fortress, to protect her, and her mother. Later, after the accident, it became a haven as well."

"Does the mountain have a name?"

"Oh, yes, but now everybody calls it Dream Mountain. Highest elevation in the South. We get snow here when nobody else does, and the rough terrain limits accessibility."

"How do you get out when the roads are iced in?"

"I have a helicopter now, but sometimes even that can't fly. Everything anyone could want is here, though. I've seen to that."

Shannon wondered if Jonathan remained isolated because he was protecting DeeDee or himself?

She didn't know how he'd react to her mentioning his face, but ignoring Jonathan's scar was not the answer. It only fed the mystique.

"Did you hear what DeeDee said about your face?"

"Yes. I heard. I wasn't aware that she noticed."

"Is it permanent?"

Jonathan bowed his head, tightening his fingers into a white knuckled fist before letting out a long disparaging breath. "Not completely," he said in a low voice. "I can't bring back my eye, of course. As for the scar, I just haven't thought about having it repaired."

"We all carry scars, Jonathan. Yours are just on the outside where everyone can see."

Shannon pulled her feet from the pool and stood. Jonathan followed. They both reached toward the stack of towels on the poolside table at the same time, accidentally touching, then pulling away.

"Sorry," he said.

"That's all right."

"I've enjoyed—"

"So have I. We—DeeDee would enjoy your company more often." She draped the towel around her just as DeeDee came rolling back into the room in her wheelchair.

"Mrs. Butter says that we can have a tea party, Kaseybelle. She's making tea and cookies. Will you stay, Daddy?"

"No, I'd better get back to work." Quickly, as if he regretted what he'd done, Jonathan Dream left the room.

Shannon had been surprised to see him. She'd expected him to follow DeeDee, but he hadn't. He'd seemed content to talk, as if they were friends. But that time had passed. DeeDee's face fell, and suddenly the lightness was gone from the afternoon.

Thinking quickly, Shannon walked toward the glass wall overlooking the forest. "Wow, those are some big Christmas trees, DeeDee. I guess you must go out and cut your own, huh?"

"I never go out," DeeDee answered.

"You never leave the castle?"

"Not unless I'm going to the hospital. My daddy

says I'm safe here. Going outside is too—tra-matic."

"What about shopping for clothes?"

"Daddy sends for them."

"What about school?"

"I always have a private teacher."

"Don't you ever play with other children?"

"I can't play, except sit-down games, and I can do that by myself."

Shannon persisted. "But what about—about going"—she was grasping here—"to see Santa? I mean, it will be Christmas soon."

"Going to see Santa is silly," DeeDee said in a quiet little voice.

"What do you mean, it's silly?" Shannon still wasn't prepared for the matter-of-fact way DeeDee answered her. When they were playing make-believe, she was free with her responses. But normal answers came as if they'd been rehearsed, and she wondered if the child were simply repeating what she'd been told.

"Silly?"

A slow anger rose in Shannon, an anger that wasn't new. Adults shouldn't make children old before their time. They should play and imagine, and anticipate. And they should have friends. Jonathan might think of the castle as a haven, but for DeeDee it was still a fortress. Even as she held Jonathan responsible for DeeDee's isolation, she excused it, for he'd thought he was doing what was best.

"It's silly asking Santa to bring something."

"Why? Everybody has a Christmas list."

"Not me. It doesn't do any good to ask for real stuff. Oh, he'll bring you toys and candy, but not the important things."

"Like what?"

"Doesn't matter, he won't bring it."

"Maybe you haven't asked." Shannon's mind was working at the problem. Perhaps a visit to Santa had been impossible in the past. She gave Jonathan the benefit of the doubt. "Have you ever written a letter to Santa?"

DeeDee considered her question for a moment, then shook her head. "Not this year."

She'd hit on the problem. "You wrote him a letter last year and asked for something he didn't bring. Did your daddy write the letter for you?"

"No, Miss Kelly, my teacher, wrote it for me. I couldn't tell Daddy. It was 'posed to be a surprise for him."

Shannon was beginning to see the problem. DeeDee had asked for something very special, very secret—so secret that she couldn't even share it with her father. Of course he hadn't known what it was, so it hadn't been under the tree.

Shannon could understand that kind of disappointment. She'd given up on Santa Claus the year she was seven. That was the year her real father had been killed in a plane crash and her nana had retired to a nursing home. It had been late November when her mother had taken her to the toy shop and told her to pick out whatever she wanted for Christmas because, "There is no way I can carry Santa Claus things on Henri's yacht."

"But, Mommie, couldn't we stay home, just me and you?"

"'You and I,' Shannon, and no. I simply can't pass up an opportunity to spend Christmas alone with Henri. And while we're talking, I'd appreciate it if you'd find something to occupy your time.

Henri doesn't like children. And if I play my cards right, by the time the new year arrives, I'll be Mrs. Henri Debierne."

Henri had become her first stepfather. He hadn't lasted as long as the toys she'd chosen. Oh, yes, she knew about getting toys instead of more important things.

"Well, I bet I know what the problem was," Shannon said, improvising as she went along. "Your letter probably didn't arrive. I heard there was an absolutely awful snowstorm at the North Pole last year."

"Really?"

"Really, and a lot of the mail got blown all the way past the pole and ended up on the Milky Way. Of course the little silver sprinkles and chocolate stars didn't know what to do with letters. They can't read, you know, so they cut them into tiny little pieces and used them for stardust."

"Ah, I don't believe that stuff."

"Well, Kaseybelle does, and she says there's one way to be certain that Santa does get your request this year."

"There is? What?"

"We'll go into town and talk to him. You can walk right up to him and sit on his knee and tell him yourself."

"I can?" Then her smiled faded. "But I can't walk."

"The walking part isn't important"—Shannon hastened to correct her mistake—"it's the telling that is. And if you can't walk, we'll take your wheelchair."

But the joy was gone. "No, thank you."

"All right. If you don't want to take your chair, then you'll just have to walk."

"But I can't."

"Your therapist thinks you can. Maybe not the entire way, but maybe we could use your chair until we get to his magic kingdom, and then, if you try really hard, you could manage the steps to walk up and sit on his knee."

"Do you think I really could?"

"I do."

"And he'll bring me what I ask for?"

"If you work very hard, I'm sure he'll say that such a good little girl ought to have whatever her heart desires."

"Then I'll work very hard."

Jonathan, who'd only gone as far as the balcony, realized that he'd been holding his breath. He thought back to the previous Christmas. DeeDee'd had a teacher for a brief time last fall, an older woman who had gone home for Thanksgiving and become ill. He remembered that before she'd left, she had mentioned something about DeeDee writing to Santa, but he'd been too caught up in finding her replacement to listen.

Damn! He'd blown that, just as he'd blown so many important things in his life. Except for Kaseybelle. Bringing Kaseybelle here had been good. He watched as DeeDee reached up and touched Shannon's hair. Her small fingers lost themselves in the fine gold mist that seemed to curl into a thousand little crinkles.

Crinkles. He looked down at his hands and saw that his fingers were digging into his palms. He unclenched them, one by one, and swore. He was becoming as obsessed with the woman as his daughter had been obsessed with the fairy.

She was so easy to be with. He wanted to touch her hair—that and more.

Lifting DeeDee in her arms, Shannon stood and walked across the tile floor. In spite of her lithe figure he was conscious of hips, and breasts spilling over the edge of the skimpy Night-Dream swimsuit. He made a note to order a more modest style.

Shannon didn't fit the image of the swimwear that his line represented. It wasn't that she didn't have the figure for it—she did. But she was more subtle, softer, hinting at passion instead of assaulting a man with her appeal.

When DeeDee laid her face against Shannon's shoulder, Jonathan felt a painful tightening of his lungs that was more than the absence of air. He was envious of his child.

Jonathan swung around on his heels and plunged down the steps and into the corridor that led to his suite of rooms. He hadn't expected a stranger to ruin his peace of mind and threaten his tenuous grip on control. Where sleep had always evaded him, now it teased, promising reprise, then swept him into sensual dreams of sharing, of touching, of the Milky Way and travels through imaginary universes—of a golden-haired woman who wore fairy shoes.

Jonathan slammed the door and turned on his stereo full blast.

Shannon left the sun room for her own quarters, satisfied that Jonathan's visit had been a positive move. Talking to him had been easier than she'd expected. Now, if she could just figure a way to get him to accompany them to cut down a Christmas tree. . . .

The night ahead would be no different from the others, Shannon realized. After DeeDee went to bed, she would be free for the evening. At home she would have spent her leisure time reading, listening to music, or sketching. But suddenly the quiet of the castle wasn't comforting.

Until that afternoon Shannon had caught only an occasional glimpse of Jonathan Dream as he watched from the loft. Now she didn't have to look up, she could feel his eyes. The sharp tingling that started behind her knees and arched upward announced his presence, and she didn't want to acknowledge her awareness. Instead she'd forced herself to concentrate on DeeDee.

But at night she found herself thinking of Jonathan, of walking with him in the snow, of the way her skin heated up at his touch. Her dreams were of her and Jonathan, and the memories stayed with her into the daylight.

Only when she was with DeeDee could she shake her growing fascination with the man. More than ever Shannon could understand why the child had grown despondent. She loved her father, but he never fully let anyone through the wall he'd built around himself. If only he'd take a real part in their sessions. But he stayed away. Shannon suspected that the pain was as great for him as it was for DeeDee.

Shannon had never suffered physical pain, but emotional pain was just as devastating. She hadn't had a Mrs. Butter to cushion her fears. She'd been alone and before Kasey had become her protector, she'd suffered from unspeakable nightmares.

And holidays had always been the very worst time of year for her. Now it was Christmas, and Shannon vowed that DeeDee would get what she wanted this year, if it was in her power to deliver it.

After dinner Shannon dressed for bed, then stood at the window gazing out at the courtyard below. Perhaps it was his very absence that made his presence more vivid. It only he hadn't left so suddenly when DeeDee had returned to the solarium. Shannon could have discussed her plan with him. She could never find a time to reach him during the day.

But Jonathan Drew was a creature of the night. And Shannon was beginning to believe that it was this place, preying on him. It was getting to her as well. If she were ever going to talk to him privately, she'd better do it quick, before she lost her nerve. Pulling on the velvet robe that Mrs. Butter had brought her that first night, she slipped out her door and down the stairs.

Now she heard the music she'd only sensed before, rolling up the open stairway. It grew louder as she neared his study.

Through the open door the sound of cymbals thundered, as if the music were bouncing off the mountains and rolling down the valley.

Shannon reached the door and paused, allowing her eyes to search the shadowy room for the source of the unrelenting wave of power that seemed forever present.

"Come in." His voice was low, yet it carried across the abrupt change to a violin's eerie wail.

"Why do you always sit in darkness?"

"I feel more comfortable. Why do you always sleep with the light on?"

Of course he knew about the lights. He had been the one who'd turned them off that first night, who'd unlocked her door and entered her chambers while she slept. She wondered how many other times he'd done so. Wondered and shivered.

"It started when I was a child," she said, drawing closer to the fire. "I'd wake and not know where I was. I learned to leave the light on—then it didn't matter." She shivered.

"Do I frighten you?"

"No. Not this afternoon in the solarium. But now, at night? Yes, I think you do," she said, letting out an unconscious sigh. "Oh, not your—your scar. It isn't that."

"Then what?"

She heard his movement and realized that he'd stood. Half mystery, half fantasy, half desire, she felt the corresponding link between them establish itself again. "Don't," she whispered, and turned to gaze at the fire. "Don't come any closer."

"I won't. I have no wish to make things difficult for you. I apologize for intruding this afternoon."

"You should spend time with DeeDee. As for making things difficult for me, I think you do—when we're alone. I don't know what to do about it. There's a kind of force that surrounds you, and it reaches out to touch me."

"It isn't me," he said, knowing that his words were a lie. "It's the isolation. You don't want to be here, and I've made you change your environment. You're being forced to form new barriers. It's understandable."

Those were just words, words that might have described himself. He'd known that she was a very private person, that she delegated all public functions and contacts to Willie Hicks. Jonathan had been amused at the man's name. Most advertising agencies were concerned with projecting the proper image, and a public relations representative in the South named Hicks was taking a risk. They made a good team, Willie and Shannon.

Willie took on the world, and she made it secure.

Then he'd come along and forced her out of her private haven into his volatile one and blackmailed her into staying.

"Yes, I don't like changes. I like my life to stay the same." But it isn't that, she wanted to say. It's you, the man. You're right about making me reform the parameters in which I exist. You're collapsing my walls, and I feel as if I'm seeping through the cracks.

Her few words were laced with uncertainty. He ached for her. He'd understood that she was shy, that she preferred solitude to people, and he'd justified his actions by saying that coming here would be a kind of seclusion that would be easy for her. He'd been wrong.

"If I've made you unhappy, I'm sorry. But you must understand that I have to make DeeDee the most important thing in my world."

"Of course. DeeDee is a very brave little girl, Jonathan. She reminds me a lot of myself when I was her age. I care about her, and that's why I've come to talk to you."

"Oh?" He hadn't dared to think that she'd sought his company for herself. Women had always come to him. He doubted the scars would change that. But he hadn't been interested in women.

Until now.

Darkness was his friend, his protector, his self-imposed prison, and his face was his penance, until now.

"What do you want to talk to me about?"

"I want to take DeeDee out of the castle."

"Why?" He'd built the place to protect DeeDee and her mother, and now himself. He'd made it secure and separated it from prying eyes and the evil of the world. This woman was asking to take his daughter away from the sanctuary he'd created?

"She needs to live a more normal life. Keeping her up here, away from people isn't good for her."

"No!"

"Oh, I don't mean some grand trip, just a normal child's outing. It's December, Mr. Dream. December is the most wonderful month of the year for children, the anticipation of Santa Claus, decorating the tree, shopping. Up here, all that's lost."

"All that was lost long ago."

Shannon looked away, planting her gaze on the fire. "For you perhaps. You can choose whether or not you take part in the world. But for DeeDee Christmas is important. She needs to believe she's normal, and I want to give that belief back to her."

She wanted to say that she wished she could give the same to him as well. It didn't matter so much for him, just as it didn't matter that she'd also found a way to hide herself from the world. But, just for a moment, she allowed herself to think about the kind of relationship two ordinary people might have shared.

He took a silent step closer. She looked so far away, so detached. He thought that she must be seeing her own ghosts in the flames. There was a sad smile on her lips.

"I want to give her the magic of Christmas," she whispered in a soft voice. "Please don't refuse."

There was a plea for hope in what she was saying, and he wondered if it was for DeeDee or for herself. Without knowing that he was doing so, he reached out and brushed her shoulder, allowing his hand to rest there for a moment until she accepted his touch.

For a moment Shannon didn't know whether the tingling in her skin was a result of the fire or the man who was standing behind her. She only knew that it pushed away the cold and made her feel warm inside.

"How can we do that?" he asked.

"By doing the things that normal people do. The first thing is a Christmas tree."

"I'll send for one tomorrow."

"No. Couldn't we go into the woods and cut our own?"

"You want to cut down a real tree?"

"Of course. We'll let DeeDee pick it out. It is all right to cut your own tree, isn't it? I mean, there aren't any laws against it?"

She turned to face him, drawing his hand with her movement so that now it rested against her shoulder where DeeDee's head had lain earlier. There was a wistfulness in her expression and a quickening of the pulse beneath his fingertips.

The only thing there might be a law against was the turn his thoughts were taking.

"I'll have Lawrence arrange it."

"Lawrence?"

"You met him at the airport. My associate. He takes care of things for me."

"No, not Lawrence. You. You have to come."

"I don't—I haven't—Dammit!" He turned away in frustration, then immediately regretted his action. He had to put a stop to his readiness to fall in with her plans. It had taken him too long to find a way to accept what had happened, to let a woman who'd only be there for a short time change everything.

"Why not?"

"Jonathan Dream doesn't go out in the daytime, Ms. Summers." It isn't that I don't want to. *I do—too much.*

She almost reached out and touched him. There was a pain somewhere beneath her rib cage that intensified with every breath. His actions were his own; she couldn't allow herself to take on the man and the child.

"We're only going into the woods, Mr. Dream. You go into the woods. I've seen you."

She was back to Mr. Dream again.

"You watch me?" His breath caught in his throat.

"Often. I see you take the dog out at night. I've often envied him his midnight companionship for a walk in the moonlight."

"You could join me." He surprised himself with the suggestion.

"No, you don't want company. I've just invited you to come with me and your daughter, and you've refused. DeeDee needs you. My presence shouldn't keep you away from DeeDee. Is it me, or—"

Her eyes were open wide, her breath coming quick and fast. Wearing the burgundy robe, she looked as if she were some chatelaine of the castle, from some ancient time. And he wanted to sweep her up in his arms and take her to his chamber, where he'd remove that velvet garment and place her on a bed of ermine and—

"—do you truly fear the light, Mr. Dream?"

"I thought you were going to call me Jonathan."

"I thought we were trying to help your daughter. Please come with us."

They weren't talking about DeeDee any longer,

and they both knew it. He was going to say no, but her "please?" was so fragile, so uncertain that his refusal died in his throat.

This time it was Shannon who reached out, imploring, laying her hand on his shoulder, feeling the sudden tension that followed. "Don't try so hard to be strong, Jonathan. Everyone needs the magic of love sometimes, along with strength and courage."

A long moment passed.

She withdrew her hand and stepped back.

The fire crackled and the light dimmed.

"And you, Shannon, what do you need?"

"I think I need to go. It's very late. Let me know what you decide, Mr. Dream."

She was halfway up the stairs when he called her name.

"Shannon, wait."

"Yes?"

"I'll arrange it. Tomorrow afternoon. We'll take the sleigh."

Five

DeeDee raced through her lessons and her exercises, not sure what her surprise would be, but trusting that Kaseybelle wouldn't disappoint her. Shannon felt herself hurrying as well. She sent her work through her computer modem, but hearing Willie's voice was more important than a machine. A quick personal call reassured him that she wasn't disintegrating and reassured her once again too.

In the kitchen Butter was humming "Jingle Bells." From beyond the kitchen door there came the sound of tromping feet and real bells.

Shannon had changed into a pair of long underwear and jeans, a turtleneck sweater, a flannel shirt, and a down-filled vest. With boots, a stocking cap, and gloves, she was ready to brave the late-afternoon snow and cold.

The kitchen door opened and the limo driver stepped inside, rubbing his hands together. "Afternoon, Ms. Summers. I think we're ready."

"We?"

"DeeDee and I."

"Oh." She hoped her disappointment wasn't as obvious to Lawrence as it was to her. Jonathan wasn't coming. Even after she'd explained the necessity of normal activities and magical dreams, he still wasn't ready to allow himself to join in the spirit of the season.

Well, so be it. The tree-cutting excursion was for DeeDee, not Jonathan, and if he wanted to hide out in his office and watch them leave, that was his loss. Shannon crammed her hat on her head and strode from the castle into the courtyard. The day was cloudy, and the threat of snow was mixed with low clouds that gave the effect of fog on the mountain.

Shannon stopped short. She didn't believe what she was seeing. Closing her eyes tightly, she waited a moment, then opened them again. DeeDee was sitting in a real, old-fashioned, straight-out-of-a-Russian-winter horse-drawn sleigh. Her cheeks were already pink, and her eyes danced with excitement.

"Come on, Kaseybelle," she cried out, "we're going to find a Christmas tree. My daddy knows where there is a perfect one."

"Your daddy?"

"Yes, Shannon, get in and cover up."

Shannon turned around. Jonathan Dream was standing at the back of the sleigh, saw in hand. He was wearing a ski mask with holes cut for his eyes and mouth, and a thick jacket with a fur collar. He'd managed to completely cover the scarred side of his face. He was dressed all in black, down to his gloves and boots. The impact took her breath away.

Quickly she followed instructions, climbing in

beside DeeDee and allowing her to pull the thick wool blanket over her knees. "Isn't it pretty, Kaseybelle? Just like on the TV."

"DeeDee, you know I'm not really Kaseybelle. My name is Shannon."

"And my name is Deanna, but nobody ever called me that, except my mother."

"Let's go!" Jonathan obliterated his daughter's final words by climbing into the sleigh and wedging himself in beside Shannon and DeeDee. He gave a cluck to the horses and snapped on the reins. They pulled away from the castle and moved briskly down the road, accompanied by the jingle of bells on the harnesses of the two horses pulling the sled.

There was no wind, and the air was moist and cold, though not unbearable. DeeDee seemed not to be aware of the temperature, chattering brightly about everything they saw as if it were all new to her. She was ecstatic.

Shannon was the one having trouble. Fitting the three of them into the sleigh meant that DeeDee had to sit in her lap. Beneath the fur coverlet, through all her layers of clothing, she could feel Jonathan's hip touching hers, his strong leg moving against hers, and his face was so close that every time she turned to answer one of DeeDee's questions, they almost touched.

"Relax, Shannon," he said under his breath. "I'm not the king of Persia. This was your idea, remember?"

"I'm fine." But she wasn't. She wasn't fine at all. In fact she was so rattled that she gave up on any conversation. DeeDee didn't seem to notice the strain, though Shannon knew she wasn't fooling

Jonathan Dream. She wondered what he was feeling.

"Daddy, isn't this fun? I'm so glad we're going to cut down a tree. Do you see any squirrels? They're probably having a tea party. Did you know squirrels have sore hands from digging?"

"No, DeeDee. I didn't know squirrels drank tea."

"Well, they do. Shannon told me. Shannon, did you know that my daddy has another horse, a very big black horse? Sometimes he lets me sit in front when he rides him."

"What's his name?"

"He's called Sinbad. My daddy named him. Can you ride a horse? Do squirrels ride horses?"

"Sinbad, a tale from *The Arabian Nights*." Shannon gave Jonathan a knowing smile. "So you do know the story of Sinbad?"

"I do," DeeDee said. "My teacher read to me about Sinbad. He was a sailor."

"About those tales, Ms. Summers. Not having read them, I'm curious, did the teller of the tales survive?"

"I don't think anybody knows."

He didn't smile, but the tone was set for the afternoon. They were sharing an adventure and were joined in the quest.

DeeDee's stream of questions rarely required answers. Jonathan was glad. He heard her chatter, but his mind was having trouble separating his attention to his daughter from his physical awareness of the woman beside him. Focusing on the horses, he managed to close out most of his unwanted reaction.

After a time the sled left the road, following a logging trail around the side of the mountain. The shaded underbrush was still heavy with snow, closing them off between walls of green and white. Shannon had the feeling that they were all alone in the world, until she heard the crash of something moving through the woods.

"Jonathan?" she called out, watching the woods anxiously.

"Something wrong?"

"There's something following us." At that moment the Malamute ran into the road, nipping at the sled in excitement. "Oh, I thought the dog might be a wild animal."

"Not Hap. He's very civilized."

"Hap?"

"His name is really Happy," DeeDee explained. "See, Miss Shannon, he always looks like he's smiling."

The child was right. With his dark mask, his open mouth, and big pink tongue, he looked very pleased with life in general.

"Hap, settle down," Jonathan said, bringing the horses to a stop.

"What's wrong, Daddy?"

"Nothing. You wanted to find a tree. Well, let's see what you like."

Jonathan climbed down from the front seat of the sled and held out his hand, first to Shannon, who hesitated for a moment, then allowed him to assist her out, then to DeeDee, who laughed and flung herself against him as he lifted her.

"May I truly pick any one I like?"

"You may pick, but remember, the horses have to drag it back, and we don't want to cut down something that's too big for them to pull."

"That's right," Shannon agreed, not at all certain any of the trees she saw could be moved by anything short of King Kong.

Jonathan took a curved handsaw from beneath the seat and handed it to Shannon. With DeeDee straddling his neck, he started off through the woods, his feet sinking in the snow to midway up his leg. Gamely Shannon followed. Drawing cartoons had never been so energetic, nor so exciting, either.

"Wait for me."

The tree DeeDee finally selected was a bit lopsided, but Jonathan assured her that if he cut the bottom of the trunk just right, it would be perfect. And even if it wasn't, it needed to be chosen. He could almost feel how happy DeeDee had made the tree.

"Really, Daddy? Can you feel that?"

"I can always feel happiness, punkin."

"You haven't called me that for a long time, Daddy, not since—"

"Here, let Shannon hold you while I cut it down."

He stopped what DeeDee was about to say, and took the saw Shannon was carrying. She propped DeeDee on her hip, stepping back out of danger.

Hap wasn't the least concerned about danger. He danced around the tree, ranging back and forth as if to say he was making the area safe for the procedure. Jonathan planted the saw against the trunk and began to move the blade back and forth. Finally, after what seemed like forever, he leaned back and peeled the ski mask from his head.

"Is it hard work, Daddy?"

"It's warm work, DeeDee."

"Does it hurt the tree, Daddy, cutting it down?"

Jonathan wiped the perspiration from his forehead and leaned on the tree. "Sometimes a thing has to hurt before it can appreciate the good feelings that come when the hurt begins to go."

Shannon wasn't sure whether he was talking about the tree or something else. Dusk was falling fast, casting eerie shadows across the forest. But Jonathan didn't seem aware of having uncovered his face, exposing his patch and scar. She focused her attention on DeeDee and the dog. Soon he turned back to his task, and moments later the tree crashed to the ground, shaking the snow from its branches as it fell.

The ski mask was back in place. The tree was soon hitched to the sleigh, and they were on their way back to the castle. Gray shadows now covered the road, and the wood creatures had grown silent. DeeDee chattered brightly for a time, then snuggled beneath the blanket, and Shannon knew that she was cold.

Moving briskly back to the main road, the horses, too, seemed ready to get to the barn and a fresh meal of hay. Lawrence was waiting at the back of the house.

"My, my, DeeDee, that's a fine-looking tree."

"I picked it myself, Lawrence. And we're going to make our own decorations. It will be just bea-u-ti-ful!"

Lawrence unhooked the tree and led the horses away as Mrs. Butterfield met them at the door with DeeDee's wheelchair. "Come inside, child. You're going to have a nice hot bath to warm you up and then some supper."

"No, I don't want to."

Shannon put DeeDee in her chair, gave her a kiss on the forehead, and ruffled her fine hair. "Go along with Mrs. Butterfield, DeeDee. You've had an exciting day."

"I've got soup with stars," the housekeeper said brightly, "and some hot yellow cornbread just for you."

"Fairy soup, Mrs. Butter?"

"Certainly, don't I always?"

DeeDee's answer was lost in the vastness of the castle walls.

"Thank you, Shannon." Jonathan came in the back door, removing his jacket and gloves. "You were right about the tree. I don't know why I never realized it."

A warm satisfaction moved through her. He wasn't immediately pulling back. His patch and his scar were exposed once more, and he didn't turn away as he usually did. She held back an urge to reach out and touch his cheek. For a moment she felt as if he were asking for comfort, as if he were waiting for her to give him a kiss and ruffle his hair.

Then he pushed abruptly past her, skimming her shoulder with his own, taking the warmth with him.

"Good night, Shannon. I'll see you tomorrow."

At the foot of the stairs he stopped and turned back. "Unless you'd like to have dinner with me?"

Did she want that?

Shannon's knees threatened to buckle. Did she want to have him renew that warmth inside her, then take it away again? She didn't think so, He'd been right about hurting. Sometimes you did have to hurt to appreciate how good it felt not to. And she was only beginning to understand what that meant.

"No," she whispered in a raspy voice, her pulse leaping across her nerve endings like Hap playing in the snow. "I don't think that's smart—I mean, a good idea."

"I never said it was a smart idea. I'm pretty damned sure it isn't. But good? That's another story." Then he was gone.

The next afternoon the Christmas tree appeared magically in the small parlor. DeeDee insisted that Shannon come and approve the spot where Lawrence had placed it.

"It's perfect, DeeDee."

"Mrs. Butter and I are going to make popcorn and string it like tinsel ropes for the tree. And my teacher let me cut stars from red and green foil paper. And we're going to decorate the tree tonight, after supper. We're all going to have a July picnic on the floor. Mrs. Butter said so. You and me and Daddy. And we're going to have sandwiches and cookies and little potatoes that curl up like corkscrews, and there'll be lights and—"

Shannon could believe the child was repeating Mrs. Butterfield's conversation almost verbatim. A smile and nod of agreement were all that were required in response.

DeeDee had been working very hard with the therapist, and her legs were becoming stronger every day. Though walking up to sit on Santa's knee, even with her leg brace, might still be too ambitious, Shannon was certain that by the time the trip came, DeeDee would be ready to rely on the wheelchair if need be.

As for Jonathan Dream sharing their meal and helping with the tree, Shannon was less sure. He'd gone to get the tree, but she'd shamed him into it, and he hadn't been anywhere around his daughter today, as far as Shannon could tell. A casual question of Mrs. Butterfield, and she learned that he'd been tied up with business. The limo had brought several men to the castle and then taken them away again.

And the addictive telltale shiver that told her he was watching had been absent.

Perhaps it was just as well. The trip to get the tree had shown her that they were too volatile, setting each other off simply by coming together. Shannon had once owned two statues, a pair of ice skaters that were magnetized. If they came together properly, they kissed. But if their poles were reversed, they whirled around and moved away from each other.

Maybe she and Jonathan shared that problem. He was North and she was South, or maybe they were both the same. What, she wondered, would happen if they ever struck the right pose?

"Oh, and Daddy is going to order us new dresses for Christmas," DeeDee chattered on. "I told him that we should have red. I like red, don't you?"

"Yes. I like red very much. I always did. I never had a red dress when I was a little girl."

"We could wear red tonight, for our July picnic. Mrs. Butter says that people wear, red, white, and blue to celebbb—"

"'Celebrate,'" Shannon supplied.

"What do people celebrate on the Fourth of July?"

"Our freedom from English oppression."

That concept seemed too much for the little girl. "Hmm—Do you have something red to wear, Shannon?"

"No, I don't think so. The only red garment I have is my robe."

"That will be good," DeeDee agreed solemnly. "I'll wear my long white nightgown, and Daddy can wear his blue pajamas. I'll go and tell him right now. We'll celebrate our freedom from—o—o—possums."

Shannon started to correct DeeDee, but she'd turned her wheelchair and was gone in a flash of excitement. It didn't matter anyway. Freedom was freedom, and maybe little freedoms were as important as big ones. DeeDee deserved a celebration. Even if she wasn't totally there yet.

While she dressed for the picnic, Shannon talked to Kasey. Their imaginary conversations were a long-established habit that reassured and calmed her.

"He's just a man, my employer. If I were more experienced, I wouldn't be reacting this way. In a month I'll be gone and all this will be a—dream."

Shannon took the dark-red velvet robe from the closet and considered what she'd wear beneath it. The lace-edged sleeves of her flannel nightgown didn't fit the cut of the robe, yet wearing only her underwear would be uncomfortable. Finally she opened the bureau drawer containing the Night-Dreams lingerie. Did she dare?

The white gown would have been her choice, but the sheer neckline was too high. Jonathan would see it and might misinterpret what she'd done. The red gown clashed with the robe, leaving only the black, slinky garment. It had full shoulders that couldn't slip, a handkerchief hemline that wouldn't show beneath the long, full skirt, and a plunging neckline that would be hidden by the fitted waist of the robe.

She carefully brushed her long hair, catching a swatch and pulled it behind one ear, where she anchored it with a sprig of greenery and a red ribbon. Donning the golden slippers, she studied herself once more in the mirror. She looked, not like Kaseybelle, the child-fairy, but like some ad-copy model from a fantasy world.

The house was quiet as always until she reached the halfway point down the main staircase, where the peal of childish laughter echoed down the corridor. Shannon paused, willing the wild beating of her heart to still. "You're simply going on a picnic, Shannon, to celebrate freeing the possums."

"Freeing the possums?"

Jonathan stepped out of the shadows, a crooked smile on his lips. "Possums?" he repeated.

"It's a long story," she whispered, caught up in the magic of the vision. He was wearing blue, as DeeDee had planned, not pajamas, but a blue smoking jacket, cut like something a Persian prince might have worn in an old movie. It was embroidered in black and gold. He looked as if he'd just stepped from the pages of *The Arabian Nights.*

"I have all night," he answered, his voice low and tight. "DeeDee said that we were dressing up and that I should wear blue pajamas. This is the best I could do. Do you approve?"

He held out his hand.

Approve? Shannon felt the intensity of his presence, her mind fragmenting in shifting sensations of light and dark, of heat and cold. The lean planes of his face were drawn into serious contemplation. His dark brows seemed permanently arched, and his lips were narrowed into a smile that, if she didn't know better, might be amusement.

She lowered her lashes and took his hand, sighing involuntarily as they touched, then waited as the heat of their shimmering connection stilled. "I think," she said softly, "that you know you more than pass inspection. But I don't matter. It's DeeDee we have to satisfy."

"I'd hoped for your approval as well."

"Why? Surely you've had all the admiration any man would ever need."

"Not from fantasy women."

"Oh?" As he drew her down the corridor toward the parlor, Shannon knew that they were flirting, exchanging nonsensical whimsy, neither believing nor expecting to be believed. This was a night of pretending. And both acknowledged with their dress that they would play the game.

"I think that a man who designs and manufactures NightDreams must have experienced the ultimate fantasy."

"Perhaps, my mystical lady, perhaps I'm about to."

"Daddy, Shannon, look at my tree."

DeeDee was wearing a long white nightgown with lace along the hem and the neck. Her dark hair had been pulled up on the back of her head and tied with a bright red bow. She was holding a bowl of popcorn, already threaded on a long thread.

"It's beautiful, DeeDee," Shannon said, pulling away from Jonathan and dropping to the sofa beside DeeDee's wheelchair. "I thought we were going to eat first."

"Oh, we are. Instead of eating on the floor, Mrs. Butter has set a table by the window. Lawrence has a surprise outside, and when we've finished eating, he's going to turn it on."

DeeDee handed the popcorn to Mrs. Butterfield and began to maneuver her wheelchair to the side of a small table set up in the bay window on the side of the fireplace opposite from the Christmas tree.

In the middle of the table was a cheerful candle arrangement with candy canes and greenery. Little white angels held bright red napkins.

DeeDee had been right about the menu. There were sandwiches, little corkscrew fried potatoes, and for dessert, ice cream with red raspberry syrup. DeeDee hurried them through every bite of the meal.

When Jonathan had scooped the last of his ice cream into his spoon, DeeDee waved her hand against the window. "Now, watch, Daddy."

At her signal a star suddenly ignited in the top of a tree at the edge of the woods. In the darkness it glowed like a beacon.

"Ohh, Daddy, isn't the star beautiful?"

"The star is beautiful, punkin."

"And he'll be able to see it, won't he, Shannon?"

"Who?"

DeeDee ducked her head and mumbled the words. "Santa Claus. I want him to know exactly where I live, else how will he be able to bring what I want most of all in the whole world?"

Jonathan stood and lifted his daughter in his arms, and the two of them stared out at the cold night sky. "He'll see, darling, and he'll bring it. Tell Daddy what you're going to ask for."

"Nope. Has to be a secret. Won't bring it if I tell."

"Of course he will, darling."

"He didn't last year. I told my teacher and she wrote it down and he never brought it."

"I know, that's why I want to make sure he knows in plenty of time," Jonathan said, making up his plea as he went. "Sometimes Santa gets very busy and loses lists."

"Not this year, Daddy. Me and Shannon are going to his castle to talk to him. He'll know, 'cause I'll tell him."

Aghast that her plan to spur DeeDee into working hard was about to backfire, Shannon racked her brain for a solution.

"DeeDee, maybe you'd better practice what you're going to tell Santa. Pretend your daddy is Santa and tell him what you want."

"Nope, it's a s'prise. Now, Daddy, we have to decorate our tree."

Jonathan gave Shannon a helpless look and turned away from the window.

The tree wasn't exactly straight, and with DeeDee's limited access, the bottom was heavy with ornaments. But when Mrs. Butter turned off the lights and Jonathan plugged in the tree, a chorus of *Ahhhs* was sweet music to all their ears.

"Now, Daddy," DeeDee said, "put the popcorn around the tree and we'll be done."

DeeDee held one end of the rope while Jonathan wound it around the tree. Then he stood back and pronounced, "It's the prettiest tree I've ever seen."

"Anybody for some hot chocolate?" Mrs. Butterfield wheeled a small cart in the door and began to pour the hot, sweet liquid into small white Christmas cups.

Jonathan sat in the big easy chair and sipped his chocolate. "Now what do we do, sweetheart?"

"Shannon says we sit in your lap and listen to Christmas carols."

"Oh? That sounds intriguing."

"Shannon says that DeeDee sits in Daddy's lap," Shannon said as she slipped off her shoes and tucked her feet beneath her on the couch. She leaned her head back on the thick pillows and watched Jonathan and his daughter. Before long DeeDee's eyes were drooping.

Shannon wondered what DeeDee's mother looked like. There were no pictures in the castle, either of Jonathan or of his wife. DeeDee's dark, silky hair was the same as Jonathan's. Where their hair touched, they blended and, except for a hint of silver along Jonathan's temples, Shannon couldn't tell where one ended and the other began.

They were both beautiful. Both special. Both in need of loving and being loved.

Just like her.

The record ended and Jonathan opened his eyes. For a long time he watched Shannon. She knew he was watching. She could always tell.

"Thank you, Jonathan," she said softly. "DeeDee will remember this always."

"So will I. I don't have many memories like this. Do you?"

"No, my Christmases were very different. Sofia tried, but she didn't understand. There were always presents and people, too many people. They came on Christmas morning and throughout the day. I didn't know any of them, but my mother thought it was terribly important to have people around her on holidays. Somehow it measured her success and it made the loneliness stay away.

Sometimes I think she worried so much about being alone that she drove everybody away."

"But you like to be alone too."

"I always thought so, but this was nice. This was almost like a real family. Thank you for including me." Shannon stood up. She'd gotten stiff sitting there in the half-darkness. And sentimental. It wouldn't do to let her employer know how deeply she'd been affected by that belonging.

"Thank you, Shannon. For being here."

Jonathan stood and followed her from the room, stopping in the doorway as DeeDee roused. "Daddy, is our tree the most bea-u-ti-ful in the whole world?"

"Yes, it is."

"I thought so."

She laid her head on his shoulder and went back to sleep. Together Shannon and Jonathan climbed the stairs to the second floor. As they reached the turret, Jonathan paused. "Shannon?"

"Yes?"

He didn't answer. His arms were filled with a little girl in a white nightgown. His heart was spilling over with emotion. His mind was treading in dangerous waters.

"Please tell me . . ."

"Of course I will. What do you want to know."

"Why were we celebrating our freedom from possums?"

Six

Only a soft light glowed from the lamp beside her bed. Shannon, still wearing the burgundy robe, was standing by the window, looking out at the star below in the woods. It made the woods look as if they'd been sprinkled with diamonds. The scene was so beautiful that she felt tears gather in her eyes.

What was happening to her? For so long she'd stayed away from people and commitment. There'd only been Willie, and he understood her fierce need for privacy. He'd respected that and made it possible for her to live the life she wanted and still be a part of the outside world.

Now, in a few short days, this lonely, powerful man had torn away the trappings of her world and thrust her into one where she didn't belong. She couldn't allow herself to learn to care for his child, or him. Her stay was temporary, and learning to care would hurt her. Shannon knew about caring and having that kind of love discarded like a change of clothes.

No, she couldn't let herself feel anything. But she had. The events of the evening had crept into her mind and settled there like a drug that could become addictive. Sitting there, in the glow of the decorated Christmas tree, with DeeDee in Jonathan's lap and the Christmas carols playing on the stereo, she could, just for a moment, believe that she belonged.

The night was clear and hauntingly beautiful. Even the coldness of its beauty didn't melt the look of warmth in Jonathan's eyes when he'd left her earlier. Now she was restless. If it wasn't so late, she'd slip back down the stairs and walk in the snow. She'd stop by Jonathan's room and ask him if he'd go with her, if he'd—

When she heard the light knock on her door, she thought she was imagining it. Then it came again.

"Shannon, it's me."

Shannon opened the door. "I thought you could enter any time you like."

"I could, but I'd rather you invite me in."

She could barely talk, her lips were shaking so. "Why are you here, Jonathan?"

"I didn't want the night to end. Do you?"

"No," she whispered, and knew that she'd been waiting for him to come to her.

"Do you know what you're wearing in your hair?"

"My hair?" She tried to focus on his words. "A ribbon?"

He stepped into the room, closed the door, and leaned back against it. "Such lovely hair," he whispered. "I'm glad you don't restrain it. I like the way it surrounds your face with gold. You look like sunshine."

She felt as if she'd died, as if all the air had been sucked out of the room and his voice was reverberating inside the vacuum. "What about my ribbon?"

"Not the ribbon," he said, taking a step forward, "the sprig of green you've tied it around."

"No, I don't know. Mrs. Butterfield gave it to me, from the arrangement she was making for the table."

"Dear Mrs. Butter. I wonder if she knew what she was doing? Yes, of course she did. She always knows."

"So, I'm a California girl. What is it?"

"It's mistletoe. Do you know what happens to a woman who stands beneath the mistletoe?"

She didn't know anything at that moment. And if she had, she wouldn't have been able to repeat it. She simply stared at him, watching him materialize from the darkness. Sunshine, she thought, sunshine turned darkness into light.

"She's asking to be kissed."

Her lungs were burning. The glow inside her had flared up with such heat that she wondered why he couldn't feel the sizzle. Closer he came. More severe, more intense were the lines in his forehead. She reached out, holding up her hand as if to ward him off, then felt the fabric of his jacket meld with fingertips that unbuttoned and touched the heated skin beneath.

He groaned. "I told myself I wouldn't come here again. I told myself that you'd soon be gone and you'd take the yearning with you. I told myself that touching you would be wrong. But you got inside my mind and messed up all my rules."

He placed his hands on either side of her face and held her, allowing their bodies to acknowledge the heated longings restrained by the boundaries of mind and the clothing. Then slowly, without closing off their vision, he lowered his head.

Lips touched. Lips parted. Lips gently asked, and took, and promised more. She sighed. He groaned. Desire acknowledged desire and became fierce in its demand.

"Shannon," he whispered, and gave in to the need to touch her hair, exalting in the silky feel of it as he wound it through his fingers. He knew that this woman was fragile, some precious gift that had come to him unexpectedly, a gift he didn't merit.

What could he offer this woman who deserved all a man had, when he had nothing left to give? His fingers stilled, and for a moment he could hear her breathing in the silence.

"Jonathan? What's wrong?"

She felt as if she could read his mind, so closely entwined were they, two people who sought solitude and yet needed not to be alone; who hid their needs from the outside world but couldn't conceal them from each other. "It's all right," she said, touching his face with her hand. "It's the magic. We're caught up in it. It isn't real. I understand."

But he didn't respond.

"You'd never hurt me, Jonathan. I'm not afraid of you."

He pulled back and looked down at her, her blue eyes clear and beautiful in the half-light of the lamp. "I've heard it said that the eyes are windows to the soul," he murmured. "How can it be that in yours I see such beauty and so much pain?"

"I don't know," she answered as honestly as she dared, "but if this is true, then half of you is concealed, and the other half remains in the shadows. Come into the light, Jonathan."

He turned his head away.

"No." She caught his face and forced him to look back at her. "I understand that you do not wish me to know, but I want to touch what I cannot see."

With her hand she rimmed the edges of his angular face, outlining the narrow edges of his clenched lips and moving up his nose to his brows. Across one eyebrow, she followed the tie of his patch across his forehead, drawing a line of heat around the edges of the material.

"Now, as an artist, I've committed you to memory."

"And as a woman?" he rasped.

"I don't know how to do that, Jonathan. Please," she whispered in a voice so low that he had to lower his head to hear. "Please, teach me."

He didn't stop to think. Instinct and a terrible, burning, selfish need took away all reason. He'd thought there would never be a second chance for him to feel with his soul. But this magic moment had come unexpectedly and unbidden into his life.

He kissed her, slowly and tenderly, feeling the trembling of her response and the shyness of her tentative touch beneath his jacket. Between kisses the buttons on her robe were unfastened, and it fell to the floor around her feet like a velvet pool.

"Sweet heaven," he said as he allowed his eyes to sweep over the black nightgown. "Our research department is wrong about the women who wear black. You're a goddess from the sun who caught me in her spell."

"Oh." Shannon looked down at her body and groaned. "I didn't expect you to see. I needed something under the robe. I'm sorry. It isn't me."

"Sorry? You're sorry that you're wearing Night-Dreams?"

"Yes. I mean, I don't want you to think I'm something I'm not."

"Ah, Shannon, you are so special. You are unique among women. If this gown makes you uncomfortable, it's gone." And he caught the hem of the gown and swept it over her head, capturing her cry of anguish with his lips and turning it into one of passion.

"I'll design something just for you, Shannon," he whispered between kisses. "I'll take the gold of the sun and the silver of the moon and give them to you."

She lost her last measure of reality as he stepped away, removed his clothes, then pulled her close again. They seemed to fit together as if she'd designed her curves to fill the planes of his body. And the connection of heat came as swiftly and strongly as it always did. She let her head fall back limply, unable to support her fluid limbs any longer. And she felt herself being lifted in arms so secure that she knew she would be safe.

As he lowered her to the bed, he whispered, "Don't be afraid, Shannon. I'll be gentle."

He leaned over her, looking down in the pale light, resting his body on his elbow. "You are so lovely. Your hair—" He spread it over the pillow, letting the wispy strands sift through his fingers. "I've dreamed of this, and you, from the first time I saw you."

"And I of you," she whispered, absorbing the intensity of the stern expression on his face.

Savage power and desire were there, but there was more. Almost hidden by his control was a vulnerability, a fear, a yearning that she sensed and understood. For it was that yearning that forged the bond between them.

Jonathan caught her nipple in his hot mouth and pulled on it. For a moment her heart seemed to stop. Then as if she were watching herself from afar, she saw herself lift her breast to him, asking for more.

She made no attempt to resist, for she knew that he would refuse to let her go. Even now he was increasing the pressure of his mouth on her nipples, burning them with his touch. Desperately she tried to hold back, afraid to follow where he wanted her to go. She heard herself making little mewing sounds, murmuring his name over and over, "Jonathan, Jonathan, please . . ."

"Soon, my love, my beautiful love," he whispered, as he caressed her with his lips and moved his fingertips to the moist heat between her legs.

They gave themselves over to the wonder of the touch and taste and the beauty of what they were feeling, to the relentless heat that burned their imprints into their skins and deep within their souls. Nothing else mattered but this time and this place, and their loving. They left their mortal world far behind.

In some dim corner of her mind Shannon knew that she should pull away. But all her life she'd known there was more, there was something waiting, something precious and beautiful. And at last she'd found it.

She opened her eyes and allowed herself to see the power of the man. He was dark and wild, and she knew that, for her, life would never be the same again. She'd been singed by his heat and marked for all time.

Willingly, with certainty, her thighs parted and she thrust against him, opening herself to that part of him that fitted most perfectly of all.

Beyond the window the snow began to fall, softly, quietly cushioning the lovers, making the world fresh and new. Inside the turret room Jonathan felt as if he were being remade.

"Are you sure, Shannon?" he asked, raising up on his elbows as he looked down at her. "I don't know that I have anything left inside me to give."

"I'm asking for nothing, Jonathan."

"No," he said with sadness in his voice, "you're wrong. You're asking for everything."

Later she lay in the darkness listening to the sound of Jonathan's breathing.

There might never be another moment like it. She didn't want to think about what had happened. She only wanted to feel and float in the wonderful aftermath of their lovemaking.

Jonathan hadn't spoken. She'd felt him stiffen in surprise when he'd realized that she was a virgin, but that had been but a momentary pause, followed by a whispered "My love." Then the world had catapulted into some great explosion of heat that had carried them beyond the edge of the universe and through the magical Milky Way, where all the fairies live.

Later he'd kissed her gently and gathered her into his strong arms, where they lay, still entwined, still connected by their ever-present thread of heat.

She'd thought he was about to leave when he

pushed himself up on one elbow and gazed down at her.

"What's wrong?" she finally whispered.

"At this moment everything is right with the world."

"Then why—"

"Why didn't you tell me that I was the first?"

"I couldn't."

"I'm very—very grateful, Shannon. That's never happened before. I wasn't prepared."

She didn't know what to say. He sounded so stern, not at all happy, as if he didn't quite know what to do with the knowledge. So she lay silent, looking up at his strong face.

"Why do you keep looking at me?" she asked.

He might have answered her honestly and said how very beautiful she was, how humble he felt, but those words were too new, too revealing. He couldn't get them out. He was afraid of making the same mistake twice. Suppose he'd given her a child? He thought he was being careful before. This time he'd never even considered the possibility. That loss of control was unsettling.

Always he'd been in control. Now he was overwhelmed, and he knew his concern was frightening her. What had happened was done and couldn't be changed. She didn't need to share his fears.

"I guess," he finally said with a forced chuckle, then realized that it was more real than he thought, "I guess I'm still trying to figure out what all this has to do with being freed from possums."

She relaxed, feeling the tension flow out of her. It was going to be all right. He didn't regret having made love to her.

She smiled, following his lead. "I don't believe I'll

tell you about the possums just yet. I think I like the way you ask questions."

"Do you?" Unexpectedly he planted a light, happy kiss on her lips, a kiss that deepened instantly.

"Is that a question?" she finally asked, her voice breathless from the kiss.

Right or wrong, he rationalized, what was done was done. Repetition couldn't make anything any different.

"A question? Oh, my love, you bet it is."

When Shannon woke the next morning, Jonathan was gone. In his place was Kaseybelle, the doll who'd been her lifelong companion.

For so long the only thing that had stayed constant in Shannon's life had been Kasey. The imaginary child, who had been her only friend and confidante had eventually become her livelihood. And Shannon had poured all her love into Kaseybelle the Chocolate Fairy. Now Jonathan had brought a different kind of love.

Love. That thought took her breath away. Could she be falling in love with Jonathan? No, she didn't want to fall in love. Every time her mother had fallen in love, she'd seemed to get a little crazy, and Shannon had always been the one to catch the brunt of her disappointment when the love went bad.

And it always had.

Shannon stretched and felt something rough scratch her neck. Pulling back the covers, she found the sprig of mistletoe caught by its ribbon in her hair.

Mistletoe. Suddenly the bad thoughts disappeared. Until now she'd never understood the frantic abandon that had compelled her mother. Shannon hadn't expected last night. Being with Jonathan was like a fantasy, and even if she never had that fantasy again, nothing could take the magic away from her. She captured the sprig in her hands and closed her eyes, willing all her doubts away.

The smell and feel of Jonathan was everywhere. She'd never be able to erase it from her body, or her mind. For one special moment she'd let go of the past, the restraints she'd always placed on herself, and she'd let herself feel.

Shannon lay still, warm beneath the covers, allowing herself one last moment of remembering while she was still safe from the self-recriminations that were sure to follow. She didn't know what would happen now. She'd learned not to expect anything make-believe to last. She'd lived out her fairy tale come to life.

And now it was morning. And Jonathan had gone.

She was alone.

Though she knew it was a temporary thing, the feeling had been exquisite. Because of her mother, she was prepared for the pain of its ending. She'd watched her mother climb to the height of excitement and expectation, then fall just as swiftly into a deep valley of despair.

With that thought, the doubts came quick and hard. And she was forced to face the truth. No matter how wonderful it had been, last night had been a mistake. Allowing Jonathan to make love to her was the last crack in the walls of her solitude. She'd given him the power to hurt her, and only she knew how devastating that kind of hurt could be. It had taken her years to get over her mother's casual neglect of her and even longer to get past the emotional pain of her mother's final rejection.

She ought to leave now, before the bond between her and Jonathan became any stronger. She ought to, but the connection would still be there. Even now she felt the constant thrumming that tied her to him. The words from some old song flitted through her memory, something to the effect that the singer had stayed too late at the fair. She might as well get up and face the aftermath of the night before, face Jonathan Dream in the light of day.

Even thinking about him brought a flush of color to her cheeks, and she hurried to wash her face and brush her teeth. She braided her hair and tied it with a bow. There was a reserve about her as she selected a pair of tailored navy pants and a bulky red pullover sweater. Warm socks and a pair of ankle-high boots, and she was ready to face the day.

The breakfast room was empty, so she proceeded on to the sun room, where DeeDee was busy with her tutor. In the kitchen she found Mrs. Butterfield cutting up dried cherries and pineapple for a fruitcake she intended to bake later.

"Good morning, Shannon. My, don't you look—energetic today. Did you sleep well?"

"Ah, yes. I did."

Shannon poured herself a cup of coffee and uncovered the warming oven where Mrs. Butterfield always left a pastry or biscuit. This morning she found two blueberry muffins, already buttered. Helping herself to one, she walked across the kitchen and peered out the back door.

"The snow seems to have stopped."

"Thank goodness. It's like one of DeeDee's Band-Aids. It covers up the booboos, and then it melts and makes everything worse than before."

Shannon debated the wisdom of her next question, but knew she couldn't plan her morning until she had an answer. "Have you seen Mr. Dream this morning?"

"Not since first light. He came down bright and early, whistling. Swallowed his breakfast whole and sailed out the door. He and Lawrence left an hour ago."

"Oh." She didn't want to admit how disappointed she was. Of course there was no reason for Jonathan not to leave the house. His life didn't stop just because he'd spent the night in her bed. He probably hadn't even thought about it this morning. After all the women he'd shared a bed with, why would he think their time together was special?

"Jonathan told me to tell you to be ready. He is taking his two favorite ladies out to dinner tonight. He said you were to put on your dancing shoes."

"Out? Jonathan is taking us out?"

"Well, I don't know that he actually meant out. Sometimes he has Lawrence bring in something special. And now and then he flies to that place he calls Dreamland in Vegas."

"What place in Vegas? Have you been there?"

"Not me. That's where he used to have all those wild parties and those DreamGirls. They were the women who modeled for him. I don't go there. It's not my kind of thing."

"DreamGirls?" Those women? Shannon had managed to put her employer's former life-style out of her mind. But that couldn't be. He was Jonathan Dream, and she would never be one of those girls. There was no point in kidding herself.

For the rest of the day Shannon had trouble concentrating. Her latest ad copy didn't flow right. She turned her attention to giving instructions to the television production company about the episode that took Kaseybelle to a castle on top of a mountain to visit her friend, Deanna. DeeDee would see the connection right away, and she'd be so excited.

Shannon implored them to do a rush on this story because she wanted it to show DeeDee that a person could overcome fear. The producer agreed to substitute it for the episode he was currently working on, if Shannon would help with the drawing. She agreed. Next she called Willie, who refused to let her get off the phone until she explained what had brought on her sudden change of heart about staying.

"I know something happened, Shan, I can tell by your voice. I don't have to be there to know. Tell Willie the truth. Do I have to worry about you and the Big Bad Wolf?"

"He isn't a wolf! Jonathan Dream's a perfect gentleman."

"And he hasn't tried anything?"

"Of course not."

"Why don't I believe you, Shannon Summers?"

"All right," she confessed with a nervous laugh. "He did kiss me. But he didn't force me. In fact, Willie, I kissed him back. It was . . . nice."

"Nice!" Her old friend and business partner shouted. "I shouldn't have let you go off up there without me, even if that associate of his did promise to keep an eye on you."

"What associate?"

"The man with the patch, John Drew. I think I trust John, but I don't trust Jonathan Dream as far as I can throw him, and you know that I can't even hit that alligator-mouth basketball goal you hung on my door with my sponge ball from three feet away."

For a moment Shannon almost told Willie that John Drew and Jonathan Dream were the same person, but she remembered her promise. If Jonathan wanted to hide behind his associate, she'd protect him. "Willie, don't worry. I'll be home in less than two weeks. I'll be safe until then, I promise."

But would she? She was only beginning to realize what it meant to open Pandora's Box. She might not be a DreamGirl, but she was in the castle and she'd already learned that she couldn't refuse Jonathan anything.

"If you don't mind my saying so, Jonathan, I wonder if you know what you're doing?" Lawrence was leaning against the fender of the limo, watching Jonathan and the mechanic fussing over the bright-blue helicopter Jonathan had bought the previous year.

"We're just getting this copter ready to fly."

"And where are you flying it?"

"I thought we'd go to Fantasy World. I've made arrangements to have the park opened just for us."

"For who? John or Jonathan?"

"Does it matter?"

"Perhaps not. But Fantasy World is on top of a

mountain. There's snow on the ground and it's night. Don't you think it's a little cold for that?"

"Of course it is, that's why I'm getting everything ready. We'll go up by helicopter. The pilot can land right in the middle of Ghost Town. We're being met by Santa's snowmobiles. There'll be battery-operated portable heaters and hand warmers and fur hats. We'll have our own private party."

"Why don't you just drive down the valley to Santa Land? It's open and it's in a heated building."

"You know that Jonathan Dream never goes out in public," Jonathan snapped. "DeeDee wouldn't understand my deception. What do you think would happen if some nosy person started asking questions about what happened? No, I won't subject DeeDee to that. I've kept her safe and I'll keep on doing so."

"That's not exactly what I meant when I asked you if you knew what you were doing. I was referring to Shannon Summers. She's not like Mona, Jon. She's very fragile. This could be a mistake."

"Dammit, Lawrence, stop reminding me. I know she's not like Mona. And I certainly know what a tragedy Mona was. I knew it then, and I live with it every day of my life, every time I look in the mirror. No, Shannon is good and . . . special."

"So, we're going to play for a while, then what? Do you really think that she'll say, 'Night-night, Jonathan. It's been fun. See you around.'"

Jonathan stopped tinkering and leaned forward, resting his forehead against the copter. "I guess not. But, dammit, it isn't fair. I did the right thing. I can't change what happened. Aren't I entitled to a life?"

"Certainly, my old friend. But this time do it right. Don't let the hormones harness you. If you want this woman, be honest about it, and be honest with her. Tell her the truth about Mona."

"That wouldn't be right."

"You pretend to be your own assistant, yet your conscience won't let you tell the truth about Mona."

"It's because of my conscience that I can't."

"Just remember, Shannon is a nice person, and much too sympathetic. I have the feeling her life hasn't exactly been a bed of roses. She's a lot like you, alone and vulnerable. If you screw things up, you could have a lot more on your conscience than a woman strung out on drugs and a little girl with mangled legs. Don't hurt her, Jon."

"What makes you think I'll hurt her? What makes you think this is anything more than a business relationship?"

"You, Jonathan. How many times have you decked yourself out like a Ninja and cut down a Christmas tree? How many times have you invited a woman out for an evening and brought your daughter along?"

"Shannon thinks that DeeDee ought to get out more. This is for DeeDee."

"And what about last night, was that for DeeDee?"

"Last night?"

"Last night. You weren't in your room."

"How do you know? Were you checking on me?"

"You mean aside from the fact that this morning you looked like the cat who swallowed the canary? No. I know you weren't in your room because you failed to flip the lock switch on the doors and sometime after midnight Hap walked in the front door. That set off the alarm, and I went to check on you. You do remember the reporter from that tabloid who managed to get on the estate, don't you?"

"Yes, I remember. Apparently I didn't close the front door tightly and I forgot to lock up. Thank you, Lawrence."

Jonathan didn't hide the smile on his face. He didn't try to play games. He'd done too much of that in his life.

"Your sudden memory loss wouldn't have anything to do with Shannon, would it?"

"Stay out of it, Larry. You're not my father."

"No, but when I'm not being your chauffeur, or your butler, or your personal secretary, I'm your friend. What's happening, Jon?"

"How the hell do I know? I like her a lot. I tried, but I can't stay away from her. I'm going to let it go and see where it takes me."

"I was afraid of that."

"You look just like the Snow Princess in my fairy tale book, Shannon."

"So do you, DeeDee, just like Kaseybelle in the adventure she has when she goes to the scary castle to spend the night with her special friend."

"You mean like our castle?"

"Indeed I do. And she's very afraid. She has to sleep in the tower room, and she's never done anything like that."

"The television Kaseybelle is afraid of the castle?"

"No, she's afraid of the dark. But she learns to face her fears, and everything turns out fine."

"Ah, I don't believe that Kaseybelle is afraid of

anything. Besides, how can sleeping in the tower make everything turn out right?"

"It's magic, DeeDee," Lawrence said as he tucked in her blanket. "All you have to do is believe in magic."

"Oh, I do," DeeDee responded happily. "Isn't this going to be fun, Shannon?"

They were dressed in voluminous white fake-ermine capes and hats. Their hands were tucked into fur muffs, and their legs and feet were covered by blankets of fur. Lawrence had driven them to Jonathan's private airfield and put them into the helicopter, whose whirling blades were already blowing snow across the runway.

"Where's Daddy?"

"Right here, punkin." Jonathan pulled himself into the seat opposite the pilot and closed the door.

"Daddy's wearing fur too.

Tonight he'd pulled his hair back and fastened it with a dark ribbon. On his head he was wearing a Cossack's hat that matched his fur jacket. Except for the hat, he looked the same as he had that first night when Shannon had watched him from her window. And the connection was even stronger.

"That I am," he answered his daughter, planting a kiss on her cheek. "We want to stay warm. It's going to be very cold where we're going. Are you wearing your long johns?"

She giggled and buried her head against Shannon's shoulder. "Daddy!"

"And you, my fairy queen," he turned his gaze to Shannon. "I hope that you're dressed properly for our adventure."

"Absolutely," she answered as she tried to be heard over the sound of the engine revving up to lift off. "Where did you get these wonderful clothes on such short notice?"

"Once we shot a magazine spread here. The fur coats and hats were used in the shoot. Lawrence had packed them away in the attic. I thought my ladies would enjoy dressing up for our trip."

My ladies. She liked the sound of that. "I'm afraid to ask where we're going."

"You wanted to take DeeDee out of the castle. We're going to Fantasy World. We're leaving reality behind and flying on our magic carpet."

"Magic carpet?" Shannon questioned.

"I'm reading *The Arabian Nights.* Don't worry. So far, I'm being entertained, so the storyteller is safe."

The fantasy was established. The promise of joy was there, in the smiles they exchanged. Jonathan had created a lovely adventure, and Shannon left all her doubts behind.

The sound of the helicopter made talk difficult. Shannon contented herself with the thought that Jonathan had found a copy of *The Arabian Nights* and read it. She knew that he didn't indulge himself in that kind of reading, and it made her feel warm inside.

In no time Jonathan's pilot landed the helicopter in the middle of a deserted snow-lined street of a western village. There were no gunfighters, no saloon girls inviting them in, but as quickly as the blades slowed, they heard the sound of an engine.

"Look, Shannon, snowmobiles."

Moments later Shannon had been installed in one of the vehicles with a driver, while Jonathan drove the machine that carried DeeDee. Across the theme park they flew, blades flying on the icy snow.

"First stop is the rides," Jonathan said as the vehicles came to a stop at the carousel.

"Rides? At this time of year?"

"Certainly. Bundle up, now." Jonathan climbed out of the snowmobile and placed DeeDee on the back of a fat, smiling pig. He tucked the furry robe around her so that only her face was uncovered, then turned to Shannon. "Which animal do you want, my fairy princess?"

"Me?" Shannon was nonplussed.

"Haven't you ever ridden on a carousel?"

"Well, yes, but not in a very long time."

"Shall I pick your steed?"

Shannon could only nod. By the wicked expression on his lips, she knew he, too, was remembering the last ride she'd taken, the night before.

He lifted her in his arms, just as he'd lifted DeeDee. Shannon's face flushed as he stepped onto the ride behind his daughter so that DeeDee didn't see the quick, hot kiss he planted on her parted lips.

"I've thought about that all day," he whispered.

"So have I." *And more.*

"Let's go, Daddy, my pig is getting cold."

"Of course, let me deposit Shannon here on this possum and we'll begin."

"Possum?" Shannon asked with a laugh. She was sitting on the back of a silvery white unicorn. "Do you need glasses?"

"Is that a question?"

She looked at the man standing beside her, at the ever-present yearning that transcended his stern expression, and nodded her head. She couldn't have answered any other way.

"You betcha."

• • •

In an empty theme park the lights blinked, the music played, and they rode the rides, sliding from one to the other on silver blades that DeeDee quickly called their spaceships. The park shops were open, but there were no clerks to take their money.

"Choose whatever you like, punkin," Jonathan said. "I've already paid the owners more than you'll ever buy."

Soon Shannon was carrying a bag that DeeDee filled with Christmas candy, Indian moccasins, pencil sharpeners, and other gifts that she refused to allow them to examine too closely. Shannon even managed to conceal a couple of gifts in the pocket of her fur cape.

"Are you hungry?" Jonathan finally asked.

"Oh, yes. We want food!" DeeDee answered for all.

The restaurant was a rustic inn, not in the theme park, but just outside at the entrance. With his hand resting proprietarily on Shannon's back, Jonathan carried DeeDee, and they entered the empty restaurant. There were fat couches pulled up before a huge fireplace with logs blazing. Carols played and thousands of miniature colored Christmas lights flickered, but they were the only patrons.

Jonathan removed their fur hats and cloaks, leaving them on a table by the door.

In the center of the dining room there was a table prepared for three. On a cart nearby were serving trays kept warm by small flame burners. Jonathan seated DeeDee, then he seated Shannon, giving her a gentle caress beneath her ear.

"Now, I shall serve my beautiful ladies."

From the caldrons he placed tender medallions of pork on their plates, adding slices of candied yams and baked cinnamony apples. There was milk for DeeDee and a sparkling wine for the two adults.

They ate in silence, almost as if they were in awe of the beauty of the occasion and the magic of the night.

"Is there dessert, Daddy?"

"Certainly. We have an entire tray of sweets. You may choose what you want."

He brought the tray to the table. DeeDee studied the pies and cakes, finally settling for a mound of whipped cream and strawberries, most of which she left uneaten as her energy level was finally depleted.

"I'm sleepy, Daddy."

"Well, Shannon and Daddy aren't quite finished with our desserts. Do you suppose you could curl up on that couch by the fireplace if I cover you up with your fur coat?"

"Yes, Daddy," she murmured sleepily.

Shannon watched as Jonathan settled his daughter in, then brought the coffeepot and filled each of their cups. "And what about you, Shannon, are you sleepy?"

"No, I feel as if I'm afraid to close my eyes, else I fall off this magic carpet."

"Good. I wouldn't want to lose you."

They drank their coffee, content to share the wonder of the moment without words.

"Would you like to dance?" he finally asked.

"I don't dance," Shannon said.

"Then just stand up while I hold you."

He held out his hand, and she placed hers in it. The dance floor was dimly lit. The music was soft and dreamy, and Shannon slid her arms around Jonathan's neck, lifting her face to look into his eyes.

"Do we have to dance?" she asked with a bit of devilment in her voice. "Couldn't you just kiss me without needing an excuse?"

He could, and he did—not once but many times. The lights flickered and the fire burned down. And two people joined in the enchantment of the night.

There was no more pretense when they arrived back at the castle. Mrs. Butterfield was waiting to take DeeDee. Lawrence took care of locking up, and Shannon and Jonathan strolled up the stairs to the turret at the top of the world.

Inside her room, Shannon waited. Would he stay or go?

Jonathan closed the door and snapped the lock.

"I brought you something from the park."

"You did?"

He cupped his hands around his gift. Then he turned what he was holding upside down for a moment and held it out.

He'd brought her a clear crystal ball in which there was a lovely gray-rock castle. The flick of his wrists had set off a silver snowfall that flurried to the ground in a lovely scene.

"Oh, it's beautiful. Thank you, Jonathan. I'll always remember this night, the castle, and you, even after the fantasy has ended."

"It isn't going to end," he said roughly. "And I'm not sure that this is a fantasy."

"Of course it is, Jonathan, and it will end."

But for one more night it was real, a beautiful illusion filled with love, with unspoken promises and dreams made real. Each knew that the end would come, but not yet, not yet.

Seven

A knock on the door woke her the next morning. Sleepily she forced herself back from the wonderful place where she'd been all night.

A second, more forceful knock rattled the door.

"Yes? Come in."

Mrs. Butterfield stood in the doorway, a perplexed expression on her face. "Shannon, I think you'd better come downstairs."

"What's wrong?"

Shannon started to rise, remembered that she was nude, and pulled the covers to her neck.

"It's Mr. Jonathan. He's locked himself up in the study and won't answer the door."

"Jonathan? Why?" Frightening thoughts rushed through her head. He was sorry he'd come to her room. The fantasy was over. He'd gone back to being the angry, unhappy man he'd been before she'd come. He was ill.

"I'll be right down. Try to occupy DeeDee so that she doesn't know."

"I sent her off with Lawrence and her teacher to find holly berries for decorating."

• • •

Moments later Shannon was knocking on the study where she'd first been summoned to meet Jonathan. There was no answer.

"Jonathan, it's me. Please let me in."

Still no answer.

Shannon whirled around and set off to find Mrs. Butterfield, who was in the kitchen. "You told me once that all the door locks in the house could be controlled electronically. Where is the control system?"

"In his office."

"Thanks." The office wasn't locked, and it wasn't hard to find the control panel. Jonathan had made it easy for her. With his usual precise efficiency he'd labeled everything. One line of blinking lights was identified as door locks. There were two switches. Shannon flipped the off switch and turned back to the study.

This time she didn't knock. She simply turned the knob and went inside. He was there. She knew it as she always did. He was sitting behind his desk with his chair facing the window.

"Please leave," he said quietly.

"Do you mean the room, or the castle?"

"Both. Go now, before I hurt you too."

His voice was tired and drained. She might have argued, but she'd already had the same argument with herself earlier, and she knew what he was going through. "It's too late, Jonathan. We can't erase what happened."

"I don't want to erase it. But I know now it can't happen again."

What she was hearing was clearly regret. He'd closed the door on their night of magic and was storing it somewhere inside that stoic mind. He couldn't make it go away, but he could contain it.

"Why, Jonathan? This makes no sense. Just tell me why?"

"I can't. Go, Shannon, now."

There was no room for argument. His dead voice said it all. No matter how much she might have wanted to protest, she couldn't. If he wanted her to go, she would. Sofia had slammed doors between them so many times. The acceptance never came any easier, nor was the pain less hurtful. But she'd numbed herself in order to deal with it, and she could do so again.

The lump in her throat was so big, she couldn't speak. But she could feel, and with pure determination she forced out the words, "No, not yet. We made a bargain, and I insist that you stick to it. Two more weeks and it will be Christmas. I'll stay until then—for a little girl who needs me to stay. Surely you will admit that she can't be allowed to give up."

"No, DeeDee is the most important thing in the world." That and holding Shannon in his arms again, feeling her body against his.

"Then we're agreed? Don't worry about what happened, Jonathan. It was just the magic of Christmas. Everyone has their weak moments, that was ours."

"Yes," he whispered, adding under his breath, "one magic moment."

She left him where she'd found him, sitting in the shadows, with his back turned to her.

Mrs. Butterfield was in the kitchen. This time Shannon didn't try to be subtle. "What happened, Mrs. Butter? Last night Jonathan was . . . different. Something had to have changed that. Do you know?"

"All I know is that this morning he had a telephone call. He stayed in his study a long time after that. I heard him and Lawrence shouting, but I don't know why."

"Was it about me?"

"I'm sorry. I don't know. I'd hoped that you'd be able to draw him out. He needs someone to care about him, someone other than a child."

"Apparently it isn't me," Shannon said woodenly. The enchantment had come to an end. He could make love to her, but she wasn't important enough for him to share his pain with her. She was being abandoned. She finally knew how her mother must have felt at the end of her affairs.

The next week dragged by. DeeDee didn't seem to notice the tension. Instead she worked even harder at her exercises. Finally the braces were put in place and she was allowed to stand up, holding on to the balance rail. Every day she forced herself to stand and every day she fell.

Though he continued to visit and encourage DeeDee, Jonathan Dream didn't appear on the balcony over the solarium when Shannon was present.

The house took on all the characteristics of Christmas—pine boughs, red-velvet ribbons, holly berries, and more mistletoe. Mrs. Butterfield unearthed a manger scene, which was set up on a table in the hall. Shannon managed to fill her days playing with DeeDee and finishing the castle episode for the television program. She wanted DeeDee to see it and recognize that Kaseybelle's determination helped her through the bad times. But the nights loomed endless and quiet in her perch at the top of the world.

Shannon never imagined that she could feel so lonely in a house filled with four chattering women. But now the tutor was going home for a visit, leaving only the therapist, who left at night, and Mrs. Butterfield.

Though DeeDee was growing stronger and had managed to take a few unassisted steps, she wasn't yet able to walk away from the bars. Shannon was worried. Perhaps her plans had been too grand. What if DeeDee couldn't manage the visit to Santa? Shannon's time was coming to an end. Leaving DeeDee, with her quick mind and unquenchable spirit, was going to be hard, and she suspected that it would be hard for the six-year-old as well. Even Kaseybelle couldn't help.

Shannon couldn't begin to stop the inner hurt that had brought her conversations with Kaseybelle to a stop and dried up her well of creativity for the first time in her life.

It was late afternoon, a week before Christmas, when DeeDee found Shannon sitting in Jonathan's chair staring out the window at the bare ground, mushy from the melting snow. The castle-visit episode was in the can and set for airing the week after Christmas, and she was uncharacteristically depressed. A sudden warm spell had swept up from the south, erasing Christmas from the picture-postcard beauty of the mountain.

The mountain seemed to be weeping. Maybe it was the Christmas carol that was playing in the kitchen, or maybe it was the melting snow, or maybe it was her impending departure, but suddenly tears welled up in Shannon's eyes, and she let out a soft sigh.

"Don't cry, Shannon," DeeDee said, "please don't cry. I don't want you to cry. When grown-ups cry, they die and go away."

Shannon reached out and hugged the child, pulling her into her lap. DeeDee was actually trembling. Her reaction was more than just concern. It was closer to terror.

"I'm not going to die, DeeDee. It's all right. I promise. I may have to go away soon, but I won't die."

"My mommie did. She cried and cried. She ran away and then she was dead. Please don't be dead, Kaseybelle. I love you."

"There, there. I won't be dead, and I love you too. I promise."

"Yes, you will."

This time DeeDee wouldn't be comforted. She continued to cry as though her heart would break. Why had her mother cried? And what made the child associate her crying with death?

Shannon finally reassured DeeDee, but the next morning her steps were less certain and she began to complain about the braces. Clearly something was happening that Shannon's tears had triggered. Only something equally dramatic would undo the damage.

It was time she talked to Jonathan Dream again, even if he didn't want her around.

But that idea proved to be impossible to carry out. Jonathan had left the castle with Lawrence and wouldn't be back until the next day. Whatever Shannon did had to be done quickly and without consulting DeeDee's father.

The therapist was working with DeeDee in the

pool when Shannon made up her mind. After the session was over, Shannon joined DeeDee in the study where she usually watched *The Kissy Chocolate Cartoon Show.*

"May I join you?"

"Sure." But DeeDee's answer was listless, and she paid little attention to Shannon.

"DeeDee, you were right. I was crying because I'm very sad. I need your help."

She'd caught DeeDee's attention with her request.

"What's wrong, Kaseybelle?"

Since DeeDee had found her with tears in her eyes, she'd changed from Shannon back to Kaseybelle. As if DeeDee was getting ready for Shannon to leave, as if she knew that the interlude was over and the fairy was becoming her playmate again.

"I don't want to go back to Atlanta."

"You don't?"

"No, I don't. But I'm going to have to leave."

"Why?"

"Because your father brought me here to help you walk and it isn't working. There really isn't any reason for me to stay."

Stark realization washed over DeeDee's face. "You mean my daddy is sending you away?"

"Yes. He will. Unless—"

"Unless what?"

"Unless he's convinced that you're trying. And I think the best way to convince him is for us to go and talk to Santa about this."

"Oh. But I wanted to walk into his magic kingdom. And I can't."

"I think you can, DeeDee. And I think if you learn to walk, your father will be very happy."

"And if he isn't sad, he won't send you away?"

"I don't know. But I'm going to ask Santa to grant my own special Christmas wish. Will you come with me?"

"Oh, yes. When can we go?"

"We'll get Lawrence to take us into town tomorrow."

"But I want Daddy to come. He will come, won't he?"

"I don't know, sweetheart, I'll ask."

"He'll come," she said with a sudden confident smile. "He won't want to miss me walking to the magic castle."

The music that signaled the cartoon show began, and DeeDee turned to the program.

"Look, Shannon, Kaseybelle is writing a letter to Santa to tell him what the Chocolate Stars want in their Christmas stockings."

Jonathan stood at his study window and felt the rage simmer inside. He'd never learn. Always he was doomed to repeat the same mistakes. At seventeen he'd destroyed the first girl he'd ever loved. She'd been taken from him by her family and sent away from the poor boy who would never be able to give her the kind of life she deserved.

For years he'd worked and struggled to become successful enough to go after her. When he'd finally accomplished it, he'd learned that she was happily married, to a good man who'd given her children to replace the child he'd given her, the child she'd lost.

Then Mona had come into his life, just a beautiful face, a woman who'd taken away the loneliness for a while. He hadn't understood how the pregnancy had happened, until the night of the accident when his life had ended. Three years later, just when he'd begun to believe that he could live again, the phone call had come.

The call that had destroyed all his foolish plans and plummeted him into a different kind of hell.

Shannon was up there, in her turret, directly above where he was standing. He could feel her. He could always feel her presence, and it ripped into his heart and pierced it with pain.

"If you don't level with her about Mona, Jonathan, I'm going to." Lawrence had entered the study and was standing by the door. "Mrs. Butterfield tells me that DeeDee has stopped trying to walk, that she's regressing. And Shannon looks like hell."

"You are not to tell her anything."

"All right, then I quit."

"You can't quit. I won't let you."

"You can't stop me, Jonathan. I don't intend to see people I care about destroyed. I've watched you isolate yourself from the world for six years. You were doing it for your wife and child. But since the accident you've tried to kill yourself too. When I saw you with Shannon, I thought that was over. But I was wrong. I won't watch you anymore."

"Then go, damn you. I don't need you. I don't need anybody!"

The silence behind him told Jonathan that Lawrence was gone. Lawrence, who'd been with him for nearly fifteen years, who'd been his trusted friend, his able business associate, and his family. Now all he had left was DeeDee. And he was about to lose her.

He heard the sound of Lawrence's truck moving off down the mountain. There was a distant slam of another door. Hap was barking. Mrs. Butterfield had already retired. Someone had left the castle. Who?

Shannon. It had to be her. Where was she going in the middle of the night? He didn't want anything to happen to her. He couldn't handle that. Without a thought Jonathan went after her, pausing at the kitchen door to pull on a jacket and gloves.

There was little snow to mark her path. He could only guess her direction. There'd been a full moon, but now dark clouds were looming up from the south. Shannon wouldn't know how violent a storm could be on the mountain. He had to hurry. He whistled for Hap, hoping the dog would tell him where she'd gone. But the dog didn't respond.

"Shannon? Shannon! Where are you?"

There was no answer. Only the whistle of the wind as it rose. There were only two directions a walker was likely to take, and after a time he decided that he was on the wrong path, turning back to try the other.

"Shannon! Please answer me!"

Shannon heard him the second time he called. She stopped her headlong plunge through the woods and considered what she had done. Dare she tell him what she'd arranged, tell him that she was forcing DeeDee to attempt to walk, to make her request to Santa with the possibility that she'd be disappointed again?

She couldn't be sure what his reaction would be. But she realized that she had no choice.

"I'm here, Jonathan." She stopped in an open space along the path and waited. Hap had run on ahead and was ranging through the underbrush. Behind her she heard Jonathan's approach.

"What are you doing out here?" he asked angrily. "Don't you realize there's a storm coming?"

"I guess I didn't notice. I'm surprised that you care."

"Of course I care. I don't want anything to happen to you."

"I'm touched."

There was bitterness where there'd once been warmth, the kind of uncertainty that came from being hurt and the loss of the connection that had been between them from the first.

Overhead clouds boiled up from behind the trees and covered the moon. Suddenly the woods became a scary place, and Shannon whirled around, ready to return to the castle.

"Where are you going?"

"Back inside. I don't like storms."

"Shannon, wait!" Jonathan reached out and took her arm, holding her back.

"Why? What could you possibly have to say to me?"

"Lawrence believes that I owe you an explanation."

"You don't owe me anything, Jonathan. But you're right, we do need to talk about DeeDee."

"What's wrong with DeeDee?"

"I may have made a mistake." This time Shannon's voice cracked, and she gulped in a deep breath of cold air. At that moment the rain started, half sleet and half icy droplets.

"Run," Jonathan instructed, taking her hand so that he could help her along.

Minutes later they reached the castle, thoroughly soaked and breathless. Outside, a bolt of lightning creased the sky, and the lights of the castle went out.

"Come with me," he said.

She followed him, shivering both from her damp clothes and from the thawing of the tension that had been between them. Jonathan led her through the darkness to the study. Inside, the fire still blazed, giving a rosy glow to the dark room.

"Come to the fire," he said.

She stumbled as she tried to walk toward the warmth.

"You're frozen," he said, and carried her to the hearth. "And the heat is off now since the electricity is out. Take off those wet things."

He pulled blankets from a chest beneath the window and handed her one, then began to add logs to the fire. She stood watching him. She felt numb, as if she were moving through some kind of slow-motion scene from that same Gothic novel she'd fallen into the first night she'd arrived.

"Take off your clothes, Shannon," he directed without turning. "I won't touch you. I promise."

Resolutely Jonathan continued his efforts to build up the fire, while listening for a sound that told him she was complying. None came. He stood and turned, Shannon was just where he'd left her, her eyes wide and frightened, her stance stiff and unyielding.

"Shannon," he said gently, "let me, please."

She raised her gaze as if she were waiting to be punished, and the full knowledge of how much he'd hurt her crashed over him. The part of him that had hoped he'd been imagining what he felt died. He was in love with this gentle woman, and he was destroying her.

His deep cry of anguish tore from his body as he pulled her into his arms. Moments later he'd removed her clothes and his own. He lifted Shannon and carried her to the easy chair by the fire, covering them with the blankets.

He didn't speak, only held her, allowing their bodies to create and absorb the warmth of their closeness. Her shivering slowly ceased, and she began to breathe evenly. The feel of her head pressed against his chest was right and good.

"Shannon, I never meant to hurt you. I'm so very sorry. I thought I was protecting you."

"By pushing me away?"

"By keeping my punishment from touching you. I'm sorry."

"It's all right, Jonathan." She raised her head and touched his face with her fingertips. "Really it is."

"No, it isn't. I should have told you the truth to begin with. You should have known what you were getting into. You should have had the choice."

"Tell me now, Jonathan."

And he told her about two seventeen-year-olds who fell in love and made a child. About the parents who refused to recognize their love and forced the girl to do away with the baby and leave the boy behind.

"Oh, Jonathan, I'm so sorry. How did you survive?"

"I didn't. A part of me died. So I created another Jonathan, one who couldn't be hurt. Eventually I became very successful, and the women came to me. They were temporary. And my image as Jonathan the dream maker grew. My company and my image became so integrated that I lost Jonathan Drew completely."

"But what about DeeDee?"

"I was always very careful to make certain that

there would never be another child. But something happened. When Mona told me that she was pregnant, it was as if I'd been given a second chance. I didn't know that mistake would get even worse."

"DeeDee wasn't a mistake, Jonathan. When someone loves you enough to give you a child, that love and that child must be good."

"Mona never loved me, Shannon. She only used me."

"But she gave you a child."

"A child I nearly killed."

"No, Jonathan, that was an accident. Accidents happen. People do terrible things to children in the name of love, but not you."

She wasn't talking about DeeDee. She was talking about a little girl named Shannon, a little girl who'd been treated badly. Perhaps if Jonathan knew her story, he might see what he'd given to his little girl.

She told him about her mother's terrible insecurities, about how she had used her love to manipulate the child she'd never wanted. About Shannon's being left alone, punished, and abandoned in her mother's pursuit of men and fame. Then, when the star, Sofia, began to lose her beauty, her little girl had become the caretaker and finally, when Sofia had turned to drugs and alcohol, the jailer.

"DeeDee knows she's loved, Jonathan. You've given her security. You must know how very important that is to—anyone who loves you."

"Anyone who loves me?" He saw the trust in her eyes and knew that she was talking about herself. He couldn't let her believe in dreams that would never come true.

"I understand what you went through with your mother, Shannon. I saw the same thing happening to Mona. The difference is that I was responsible for her drug use. Oh, I never took them, but I should have realized what was happening. When I discovered she was doing coke, I found her supplier and fired him."

"But you tried to help her. I know you did."

"Don't make me more than I am, Shannon. Yes, I brought her here and provided medical care for her until after DeeDee was born. But then I insisted that she stay."

"And she didn't want to?"

"By that time she wanted the drugs more than she wanted me. If I had let her go, the accident would never have happened. She might still be alive and DeeDee would be a normal, happy little girl who could walk."

"She can still be, Jonathan. That's what I wanted to talk to you about."

"I'm listening, Shannon, though I don't know that I want to let myself hope anymore."

"I've done a risky thing. You have every right to be very angry with me."

Anger was the last thing he was feeling toward Shannon. Holding her in his lap, touching her, feeling the gentle whisper of her hair against his cheek, he sensed that an unwanted web of warmth was being spun around them. He could feel the gentle swell of her breast resting on his arm, the softness of her silk underthings caressing his thighs. All the feelings he'd locked away came rushing back, and he tensed.

"What have you done, Shannon?"

"DeeDee found me crying and she became very

upset. She said that everyone who cried died and went away."

"I didn't know she knew about the crying."

"Mona?"

"Yes, she managed to find new supplies of drugs. Toward the end she switched over to crack. It was pretty bad. Sometimes she'd become psychotic and would go on crying jags. She'd cry and scream, accusing me of . . . pretty awful things."

"And DeeDee heard her."

"I thought DeeDee was too young to understand."

"I think she was. She misinterpreted what she was hearing. Maybe you ought to talk to her about what happened."

"Tell her that her mother was so strung out on drugs that she tried to kill herself by driving off a mountain?"

Shannon sat up.

"Mona was driving the car?"

"I didn't say that."

"But she was, wasn't she? Not you—Mona."

"Yes."

"Then you didn't kill her and you aren't responsible—"

"Yes, I am. I told her to get out. That I was tired of trying to help her. That she was on her own. And she left."

"You let her take DeeDee?"

"I never wanted her to. That was her final vengeance. She laughed when she told me, laughed at me. She said that DeeDee wasn't mine."

"Not yours?"

"I was a fool. I believed that the child was mine

because I wanted her. The truth was, she was sleeping with everybody on my staff."

"I'm so sorry, Jonathan."

"I wasn't. I wanted the baby."

"But—your face? How did that happen?"

"I was so shocked and hurt that I let her drive away. I didn't know she had DeeDee until I heard her screaming, 'Daddy! Daddy!'"

Shannon stared at the man in disbelief. She was shaking her head, murmuring, "No. I don't believe you meant it to happen. It was an accident, Jonathan, an accident. You didn't mean for her to die."

"But I did. For that one moment I did. Then I realized what she was doing and went after her. Just at the point that I almost caught up with her, she looked back and lost control. The car sailed off the road and landed in a ravine. The car caught on fire. I could hear DeeDee shrieking."

"Oh, Jonathan. How terrible."

"I had no choice. I tried to climb down the ravine. It was too steep. I never would have made it down if I hadn't fallen. When I came to a stop, I'd landed in a tree. That's how I lost my eye. I managed to get DeeDee out of the car, but I couldn't save Mona."

"How sad. How very sad for her. But DeeDee survived and you love her, I can see it. So don't tell me that anything Mona said about that child matters."

"But Mona was lost forever, and DeeDee's legs were broken. I never should have let it happen."

"And you've spent the last three years making amends."

The gentle assurance he'd come to depend on was there for him. She pulled his head against her breast and held him, as if he were the child and she were the parent.

"I've tried. The doctors said she should be able to walk after the last operation, but she stopped making the effort. I wanted so badly to create a pure world for DeeDee, a happy place where nothing evil could touch her. But it didn't work."

"It still can, Jonathan. All you have to do is show DeeDee that you're here for her, always, no matter what."

"She knows that."

"Yes, I think she does. But that belief has gotten mixed up with being disappointed about something that is very important to her, and now she's lost her faith. I think we all know what it means to lose our faith."

"What am I going to do?"

"Nothing. But there's someone who can."

"Who?"

"Santa Claus. Tomorrow I promised DeeDee that she and I would visit Santa. And with any luck I'll find out what it is that she really wants. Will you go with us?"

"And what do we do if we can't give her what she wants?"

"We will. I'm sure of it. It's Christmas, Jonathan. Please. You need to learn to believe."

Jonathan pulled away, his face filled with uncertainty. "This could be a mistake, Shannon. We've gotten so carried away with fairies and fantasy that we've lost touch with reality."

"No," she whispered. "DeeDee needs to believe in Santa. She needs to believe that she's going to walk. If we help her believe hard enough, she will."

"It doesn't work that way in the real world, Kaseybelle," he said sadly. "It's only in your Milky

Way fairyland that all the children's dreams come true."

Reality had come into the room. And reality brought fear to Shannon's eyes. She stood, staring at him, her face awash with pain. She wanted him to take her back in his arms, to comfort her and tell her that he'd make things right. But that would only be adding to the fantasy.

Jonathan winced. He wished he could start over, keep his child on his mountain where he could protect her. But he couldn't protect DeeDee or himself. His sanctuary had been breached by this woman. He'd fallen in love. And the cold truth was that he spoiled everything he touched. He'd destroy her just as he'd destroyed every other woman he'd cared for. His heart hurt, and he knew that it would never be whole again.

He and Shannon would never have a life together. DeeDee might never walk again. And he was about to lose them both.

Slowly Shannon wrapped herself in her blanket. Finally she turned. "You're right, you know. We've both created a fantasy to cushion us from pain. But something happened that I didn't count on. I fell in love."

"All part of the fantasy," Jonathan said in a low voice.

"Perhaps, but we'll never know, will we, unless we go back into the real world?"

"The real world destroys love, Shannon. The only chance we have is by trying to preserve the fantasy. And now that's in danger of ending."

"I don't know why you're so certain that you can't be happy, but there's one thing I do know. I'm taking DeeDee to see Santa tomorrow. If you care about DeeDee, about me, you'll come too."

"No. All I have to do is let them in, and once they start their attack, DeeDee could be permanently destroyed."

"Let who in? Why would anyone be looking for us?"

He hedged. "The reporters are always down there. Lawrence keeps them away. Once they see me with DeeDee, there'll be no concealing what happened or who I am."

He could have told her that he was more afraid that if the world knew the truth, someone might claim DeeDee.

As if she'd ordered it, the power came back on, illuminating the room. The tree lights began to twinkle.

"I think that you use that patch and that scar to hide, Jonathan, just as I've used Kaseybelle. So what if the world sees you? DeeDee loves you. She doesn't care."

"She won't know any different, until people whisper and make her feel ashamed."

"Nobody would ever be ashamed of you, Jonathan. We're leaving in the morning, about ten. I'm hoping that the line won't be so long if we go early. Come with us. Please."

"I can't."

"It's your choice."

"Don't go."

She didn't know whether he was asking her not to leave the study or not to go into town. It didn't matter. She had to do both.

Shannon put on her clothes and was gone. Outside the window the sleet changed into snow and the world turned white again.

Eight

But they didn't go the next morning, because Lawrence hadn't returned, and the snow made the roads too treacherous for Shannon to risk making the trip alone. Driving was something she did little of under ordinary circumstances. She didn't dare try it now.

After DeeDee went through her exercises, she was filled with pent-up energy. Throughout the day Shannon amused her by playing games and wrapping the presents they'd bought at Fantasy World. Shannon had managed to slip away with two small gifts, a magic wand for DeeDee and a tiny carved opossum for Jonathan.

Still the day loomed long, and Jonathan never appeared.

"Mr. Jonathan's out riding that big black horse," Mrs. Butter reported at lunch. "He's gonna kill himself or break that animal's leg the way he tears through the woods as if he's being chased by the devil."

"Like some barbarian warlord," Shannon said

softly, "who rapes and pillages a woman's heart."

He didn't make an appearance at dinner either. But the next morning Lawrence was at the breakfast table. "Morning," he said, as if he were fired and rehired every day.

DeeDee was already dressed and busily planning just what would happen once they reached the mall. "Good morning, Shannon, you have to eat quick. Lawrence is ready, and so am I."

"Jonathan?" Shannon said, and raised a questioning eyebrow to Lawrence.

He gave an almost imperceptible shake of his head.

Well before ten o'clock they were installed in the limo, and Lawrence was driving down the snow-covered road toward the gate.

DeeDee's chatter stopped. She looked out the window. "He isn't coming, is he?"

"I don't know," Shannon answered. "I think it's very hard for him. We must try to understand."

"That's all right. I'll speak to Santa Claus. He is—" Her voice wavered for a moment. "He really can bring the things you want, can't he?"

"Sometimes, but perhaps not always. Won't you tell me what you're going to ask for?"

"I'm going to ask him to fix my daddy's face so he won't be sad anymore and . . . and . . . things."

It was the "things" Shannon was worried about. Somehow she had to find a way to let Santa Claus know how important it was for DeeDee to get what she asked for. The only way that would happen was for him to pass on DeeDee's request.

Lawrence opened the gate electronically and the car moved through slowly.

Then they heard it, the sound of crashing, of the

horse as it burst through the underbrush and onto the road just ahead of the car.

"Daddy!" DeeDee let the window down.

"Jonathan, you fool." Lawrence brought the car to a stop as the horse came alongside. "You're going to kill that horse."

Jonathan slid off the horse and turned him back in the direction of the castle, giving him a slap on the rear. "Go home, Sinbad."

"Daddy, you're coming with us?"

"Of course, punkin. I couldn't let you go to the North Pole without me."

He climbed into the car, his long hair frosted with snow, his feet leaving clots of white ice on the floor mats. Once inside, he leaned back, pulled DeeDee into his lap, and rested his chin against her head. "Glad you're back, Lawrence."

Shannon was holding her breath. She had no idea what to say, how to respond to this man's unorthodox entrance. No, not unorthodox, she decided. He would always be larger than life, and his wildness was only a part of the essence of Jonathan Dream.

And then he looked at Shannon, openly, sternly. "How are you this morning, Shannon?"

"I'm fine," she said in a shaky voice. "We missed you yesterday."

"Did you?"

"Yes. Where were you?"

"I was possum hunting. Couldn't find a possum on the mountain," he said with a suggestion of humor in his voice. "I guess you and DeeDee must have freed them all." And then he smiled, an honest, genuine, wonderful smile that caught Shannon by surprise.

"Oh, Daddy, me and Shannon don't really have any possums. You're silly."

"I guess you're right, punkin. What do you think, Shannon?"

She debated about her answer for a moment, then gave way to the lightheartedness of the moment. "Is that a question?"

Jonathan's smile narrowed into a thin, serious line. "I think it is, Ms. Summers. I think it certainly is."

DeeDee insisted they sing Christmas carols to pass the time. Even Lawrence opened the partition and joined in. Shannon listened to the voices and felt a warm glow steal through her. This was the way it should be, the way a family ought to be and never was.

She thought about what was ahead and worried. Suppose DeeDee fell? Suppose she became afraid and refused to talk to Santa? Suppose the reporters really were waiting? What if she'd made a mistake?

She didn't know what had changed Jonathan's mind about coming. Nor was she certain how she felt about his being with them. She was afraid to believe that the day would be happy. Suppose it turned into a disaster?

Her fears weren't only for DeeDee, but for Jonathan as well. She'd forced him into the world, and she understood that his apprehension was as strong as her own. The connection between them had reestablished itself without her being aware. When had it returned?

Almost from the moment they'd faced each other, they'd been joined, first by physical awareness and then by mutual commitment to his child. She let out a sigh as she looked out the window.

The sun was shining, kissing the snow-covered trees with diamonds. Overhead a bright-blue sky was smeared with pallet-knife blobs of white spread across in straight, thin lines. A flash of black darted across the treetops and off again as some winged predator searched for food.

Suddenly Shannon felt an odd sense of unease, as if she were exposed, pinned down against the earth while her winged assailant stayed just out of sight. It was the unknown, she decided, and the risk she was taking. She shivered.

"Are you cold, Shannon?"

He didn't miss anything. He saw her almost imperceptible movement. She had the feeling that he was reading her mind as well. But she couldn't tell what he was thinking. Just the force of his attention turned her into gelatin, while he'd encased his feelings in steel.

"No, I'm fine."

". . . and we'll get in line," DeeDee was telling Lawrence, "and then we'll get up to the North Pole, where Santa has his magic kingdom. There will be elves who'll give us candy and take our picture. Will they take your picture, too, Daddy?"

"I don't think so, DeeDee. I don't believe that I can fit on Santa's knee, do you?"

She studied her father carefully, then shook her head in agreement. "But Shannon can. She can sit on Santa's knee and ask him to bring what she wants most of all in the whole world."

"Oh, I don't think so—" Shannon began.

"Absolutely," Jonathan agreed. "I think that she should have her picture taken with Santa just like you. Have you both been good?"

"You know I have, Daddy."

"I don't know," Shannon answered honestly. "I don't know anymore what 'good' is."

Jonathan pushed DeeDee's hair away from his face, shifting her so that she could look out the window and he could plant his gaze on Shannon. "Well, I know," he said. "You've both been good, very, very good."

The mall was crowded. It was the largest one outside of Asheville, and everyone at the foot of the mountain came to shop. Lawrence drove up to the entrance and stopped. He took DeeDee's wheelchair from the trunk and set it up while Jonathan helped Shannon out, then lifted DeeDee.

"Now you push me, Daddy, until we get in line. Then, when it's my turn, I'll stand up and walk to Santa's castle."

"Fine, punkin," he agreed, until he saw the layout and felt the anger rise. There were steps, a series of three sets of steps up to the raised platform on which Santa's North Pole castle had been constructed. "Damn!"

"Oh," Shannon whispered. "How could anybody plan such a layout?" DeeDee couldn't manage this kind of arrangement, and there must have been other children who wouldn't feel comfortable going up there alone.

DeeDee simply stared at the scene, then turned her face toward Shannon. "I don't know if I can do that, Kaseybelle," she whispered, "it looks very hard."

"It looks irresponsible," Jonathan said, swearing again.

By that time Lawrence had parked the car and joined them. "Well," he said brightly, "let's get in line."

"But, Lawrence, I don't think I can do that," DeeDee said.

"I'll bet that Santa has something worked out for just such a problem. Why don't we give the old boy the benefit of the doubt?"

DeeDee's eyes lost a little of their disappointment. "Like what?"

"Haven't a clue, little one. But this is a magic place, and I'm willing to believe in magic. What about you?"

"Me, too," Shannon said, taking the chair handles and moving DeeDee into line. She closed her eyes and gave a brief prayer for divine intervention, all the while aware that Lawrence had disappeared into the crowd.

Jonathan moved in behind her, taking her elbow as he leaned over to whisper in DeeDee's ear. "Don't worry, punkin, we'll make it to the last set of steps, then if I have to, I'll carry you up there."

"Oh, no, Daddy. I have to do it myself, or else Santa might not bring me the thing I want most in the entire world."

Instead of being apprehensive as Shannon had feared, DeeDee put her reservations behind her. She'd been told to believe in Santa, and she was ready to believe. She kept looking over her shoulder, first to the left, then to the right, as if she were checking to make certain that both Shannon and Jonathan were still there.

"Sorry." Lawrence appeared behind them. "There's no other way to get to the North Pole except up. Apparently they don't cater to handicapped people around here."

"Don't worry, Lawrence," DeeDee said. "I can do this myself. But next year my daddy is going to make sure that Santa moves where there aren't any steps."

The crowd moved slowly forward. The mall was filled with last-minute shoppers who gathered on the second floor and stared down at the North Pole below. Children cried, mothers became short-tempered, and Shannon began to worry. But DeeDee's spirit never flagged.

Finally they reached the first set of steps.

"Release the footrest, Lawrence," DeeDee directed, lifting her braces and setting them firmly on the floor in front of the chair. She stood, found her footing, and stepped up onto the first step.

Jonathan tensed every muscle in his body.

Shannon held her breath.

Lawrence had moved forward to talk to Santa's helpers, pressing something folded into the hand of the pixie nearest Santa. He caught Jonathan's attention and flashed the thumbs-up sign.

DeeDee made the second step and the third. She stopped and turned back. "Now, Daddy, you and Shannon may hold my hand."

Solemnly Jonathan urged Shannon up the steps, each of them taking one of DeeDee's hands as she'd instructed. She reached Santa's throne and allowed her father to lift her to Santa's knee. Giving both Shannon and Jonathan a strong look that told them her conversation was private, she turned to whisper in Santa's ear.

Moments later she slid from his knee and took her father's hand. "All right, Daddy, we can go now."

"What about you, young lady?" Santa asked as

Shannon scooted by. "Don't you want to ask Santa for something special?"

"All I want is for DeeDee to get what she asked for," she said, and turned to follow Jonathan as he carried DeeDee away from the North Pole.

"Then you'll make a fine mother," Santa said, turning his attention to the next child who was coming forward.

"Mother?" Surely she'd misunderstood what he'd said. But she hadn't. With a sinking feeling in the pit of her stomach, she understood what DeeDee had done.

Shannon looked around for Lawrence. She needed to have someone tell her that she'd misinterpreted what had happened. But Lawrence had stayed behind to pay for the pictures and claim the information he'd paid the pixies for.

From the North Pole they headed for the open food court, where DeeDee selected pizza for all. Jonathan found a table for the three of them and went to place the order. Shannon sat, listening to DeeDee's happy talk.

"And I told him, Shannon, and he said that he thought I had a very fine idea, and that he was sure that it would work out just like I wanted it to. Of course he didn't say 'zactly, but he knows, and Santa can bring whatever I ask for, if I'm a good girl, can't he?"

"But, DeeDee, Santa brings toys and fruit and candy. He can't make—things—happen just because we want them."

"Santa's magic, Shannon, just like Kaseybelle. I wanted you and my daddy got you. Santa will answer my request too."

Jonathan had been right. She should never have interfered. She'd made a bad mistake.

Jonathan paid for the pizza and fought his way back to the table. Shannon was studying DeeDee, listening to her conversation, but it was obvious that her mind was far away. He put the cardboard box on the table and served pieces to everyone. He and DeeDee ate, enjoying the rich cheese and tangy sauce. Shannon only toyed with her slice.

Maybe, just maybe he'd been wrong about facing the world. There was no shortage of attention showered on them, but he wasn't sure whether it was because of DeeDee or because the children recognized that Shannon was a Kaseybelle look-alike. For the first time in a very long time, he didn't feel the attention focused on him.

Until he glanced across the tops of the patrons sitting around the small tables and saw a television reporter facing a portable television camera. The camera slowly panned the crowd, reached the table where they were sitting, moved on, then came back. The reporter quickly turned to face them.

"Damn! We've been discovered." Jonathan stood, ready to grab DeeDee and flee. But the camera didn't seem to be focusing on him.

"Aren't you Sofia Summers's daughter?" the aging reporter asked, holding the microphone out for her answer.

Shannon's face turned white. Her voice tightened up so that she could hardly speak.

"Ah, yes, I am."

"I'm Noel Cross, reporter with Channel Eight News. I don't believe it. You, here in North Carolina. I was one of your mother's biggest fans."

"Thank you. We have to go now." Shannon stood, trying to bring the encounter to a close.

"And I've seen your name on that cartoon show, haven't I, the one about the fairy?" He loomed closer. "Tell me."

"No!" DeeDee screamed out. "Don't you hurt Kaseybelle!"

"Where have you been since Sofia committed suicide? I'm certain her fans would like to know."

"Now, just a minute," Jonathan interrupted, pulling Shannon into the safety of his arms. "She isn't interested in being interviewed."

"Say, don't I know you from somewhere?" The reporter took in the scar and the patch, allowing his gaze to come to a stop as recognition swept over him. "Jonathan Dream. You're Jonathan Dream. I'd heard that he'd become a recluse, but I never realized—get this on film, Joe."

Shannon let out a cry of dismay. "Oh, no! Please, don't film this," she begged. "It's Christmas. We're just enjoying a family activity."

"Family? You and Jonathan Dream are married?"

"No, I'm just a friend," Shannon answered warily. "And this man is Mr. Drew. You're mistaken."

"I'm not mistaken, lady. I have a thing about faces. Jonathan Dream and Kaseybelle. You do look like her. NightDreams and the Kissy Chocolate Fairy. Now that's a combination the world will find interesting."

Jonathan swore.

DeeDee began to cry.

The camera whirled.

And suddenly it all came back to Shannon, the wild-eyed fans, the pushing and jostling of the press, people shoving her away trying to get to her mother. Sofia would pretend to be annoyed, dragging Shannon along with little regard for her physical comfort. Yet she'd stop often enough to allow them to ask more questions. Actually Sofia loved the frenzy, basked in the attention. Often Shannon would be lost in the crowd and left behind, afraid and alone until her mother would remember and send someone for her. Then she'd be punished for worrying Sofia.

Later, when Shannon was older and Sofia was less able to handle the press, it fell on Shannon's shoulders to protect her mother and keep them away. Sometimes she hadn't known who was the mother and who was the child. She'd begun to feel as if she were losing parts of herself, that someday she'd be neither the child nor the protector, and she'd disappear completely, leaving her mother to be destroyed.

She couldn't allow that to happen to DeeDee.

Nor could she let herself be responsible for exposing Jonathan Dream to the world. He'd tried to tell her, but she hadn't listened. Now she had to do something.

Shannon began to move toward the reporter. "All right," she said softly, "if you'll come with me, I'll give you an exclusive interview."

"But I'd prefer talking to both of you. Keep filming, Joe."

"It's me or nothing, buster."

"No, Shannon, don't do this," Jonathan said in a low, threatening voice. "I'll stop him."

"Take DeeDee to the car, Jonathan. I'll join you later."

Adroitly Shannon managed to maneuver the

reporter away, allowing the line of people waiting to be served to cut them off from the eating area where DeeDee was. She hoped that Jonathan followed her directions. No child should have to undergo what she had. This catastrophe was her fault, and it was up to her to end it.

Nine

"Dammit, Lawrence, where is she?"

They'd been waiting for over an hour. DeeDee had fallen into a tearful sleep in the backseat while Lawrence and Jonathan had taken turns combing the mall, with no success.

It was late afternoon when the mall security located the cab driver who had driven Shannon to the airport where she'd bought a ticket back to Atlanta.

"Gone? Why, Lawrence?"

"Something must have happened to frighten her."

"It's that reporter's fault. If I hadn't tried to hide from the world, this would never have happened. You take DeeDee back to the castle. I'll go after her."

"And what will you do then?"

"I'll bring her back."

"And after that?"

"What the hell are you asking, Lawrence? I'll just keep her here, with us. DeeDee needs her."

"And what about Jonathan? Could it be that he needs her too?"

"No! You know I—I can't. I won't take another chance, not again."

"Sure you can, Jonathan. You're no monk and you're no jinx either. You can't let your guilt over Mona control your life anymore. Even DeeDee knows that you and Shannon belong together."

"What does DeeDee know about anything?"

"She knew to ask Santa for a mommie for Christmas."

Jonathan went pale.

"A mommie?"

"Seems she asked last year, but he didn't bring what she ordered. This year she brought her choice along so Santa would know just which one she's picked out. All she needs is for Santa to make it so."

"Shannon? DeeDee wants Shannon to be her mommie?"

"You know the answer to that question, and I think that Shannon knows too."

"What does that mean?"

"According to the pixie, Shannon told Santa she wanted the same thing that DeeDee asked for."

"But—but, Lawrence, if that's what she wants, why did she leave?"

"You're going to have to figure out that puzzle yourself, my old friend."

From the Atlanta airport Shannon tried to buy a ticket for California. She couldn't imagine why anybody would want to go to California for Christmas, but apparently it was a popular choice, because there were no seats.

An hour later she was on the first plane with a vacancy. She was headed for Charleston, where she'd stay until she decided what she was going to do. She couldn't stay in Atlanta; Jonathan would come for her.

Or maybe he wouldn't.

Why would he? They'd had an agreement and it had been completed. Willie would have the Night-Dreams account and become an eccentric millionaire.

As for you, Shannon, this time you'll walk into the ocean and join Neptune under the sea. Fairies are out. Fish are in. You can be a mermaid.

Except DeeDee had asked Santa for a mom for Christmas, and DeeDee wanted her, not a mermaid. Even if she did exactly what DeeDee wanted, there was still one problem that made the idea impossible. A mommie was not only mother to the child, she was wife to the father.

Mother.

Wife.

From the airport she made a quick stop by a mall, where she picked up clothing and toilet articles. A filmy nightdress drew her attention, and she stopped, caught by its sultry lines.

"That's a NightDreams original," the clerk said. "Isn't it the most exquisite thing you've ever seen? I understand that Jonathan Dream creates every NightDream personally."

Shannon groaned. NightDreams weren't the only dreams he created. He'd done a fine job of influencing her daytime thoughts as well. Now DeeDee, too, was ensnared in a dream. But she couldn't blame that entirely on Jonathan. She'd helped foster DeeDee's fantasy.

Emotionally and physically exhausted, Shannon checked into the Planters Hotel in the heart of Charleston's historic district.

"You're lucky, ma'am," the desk clerk said. "We've been packed lately, but everybody's checking out of here to get home to their families for Christmas."

Shannon looked around at the brightly decorated old hotel and thought about how much DeeDee would like it, about the rustic old inn where they'd had dinner. She moaned. Was she going to carry that memory around with her forever?

DeeDee.

Jonathan.

Everything about Shannon hurt. Even her eyes were dry and strained from trying not to cry. She followed the hotel clerk to her room and tipped him, immediately turning off the lights and opening the drapes so that she could see the city beyond.

She felt like her mother, looking for a place to hide, yet wanting desperately to be found. In Charleston she was nobody. She was lost among those left behind with no home and family with whom to spend Christmas.

"Stop it, Shannon, don't get maudlin. This isn't some television special, this is real life. And there are no happy endings."

She'd known from the beginning that she was taking a great risk in leaving Atlanta. But she'd had no choice. She'd told herself it was for Willie, but it had been for her, for Kaseybelle. She'd had to protect the life she'd created, both the present and the past. She hadn't been prepared for the even greater pain of leaving the castle or making a place in her life for others.

Shannon kept remembering the ride through the snow in a horse-drawn sleigh, watching the lacy flakes drift down and settle on Jonathan's dark hair when he'd removed his ski mask. The lovely trip to Fantasy World where they'd ridden the carousel and he'd kissed her. But the memory that hurt most was DeeDee's Christmas tree and the star Lawrence had put up to signal Santa.

Choking back a sob, Shannon pulled down the spread and collapsed on the bed. She still had Christmas Day to get through. Afterward she'd go back to her apartment, where she'd try to redefine her life once more.

She hoped DeeDee wouldn't be too distressed that she'd gone. But Lawrence would have told Jonathan about DeeDee's wish, and he'd find a way to explain why it couldn't come true. DeeDee knew now that she could walk. And Shannon hoped the little girl would continue her therapy and get stronger, concentrate on her progress instead of her pain.

Shannon's own pain was too great. For now she knew that what she wanted most was, just as it had always been, something she couldn't have.

She wanted Jonathan Dream to love her.

After a restless night Jonathan went to find DeeDee. Now that he knew what she'd asked for, he expected to find her more depressed than she'd been before her visit to Santa. He was wrong. Instead she was standing by the kitchen worktable, tracing the outline of her hand with a knife on rolled-out gingerbread dough.

"Look, Daddy, we're making gingerbread handprints."

"DeeDee," Jonathan began, hating himself for what he was about to say, hating Shannon for making him say it. "I have something to tell you."

"What, Daddy?"

"It's about Shannon. She's gone back to Atlanta."

"That's all right, Daddy. She's coming back."

"No, I don't think so, and I don't want you to be sad."

"Oh, I'm not. And don't worry, Daddy. Me and Santa got it all fixed." She took several steps toward Jonathan, pride in her accomplishment showing on her happy face.

"That's what I'm trying to tell you, punkin. Sometimes Santa can't bring us the things we want."

"Of course he will. Shannon said that if I worked really hard and walked to Santa, he'd be sure to bring me what I asked for. He will."

Jonathan groaned. *Damn you, Shannon Summers!* She'd accomplished her purpose in coming to Dreamland, but now she would destroy all that. There was no way that DeeDee could have what she wanted. There was no way he could give it to her.

He swung around and went into the study. "Any news yet, Lawrence?"

"Not yet."

"I can afford to buy and sell a mountain, but I can't buy a simple piece of information about where one woman has gone?"

"Jonathan, Willie swears he hasn't seen her, and I think he's telling the truth. She has a few friends, but none of them have seen her. And she has no family to turn to."

"All right, if she hasn't gone back to her old life, she must have gone somewhere else."

"If she did, she went under another name."

"Find out, Lawrence. Call in every private-detective agency in the state. Get in touch with that reporter from Channel Eight. She talked to him. See if he knows where she is."

Lawrence leaned back in his chair and glared at Jonathan. "And what will you do when I find her?"

"I'll marry her!"

"Why?"

"Because DeeDee needs her."

"You married Mona because of DeeDee, Jonathan. You never loved her, and it didn't help DeeDee or you. What makes you think that this won't end the same way?"

"Because—" Jonathan sank into a chair and covered his eyes with his arm. "Because I love her, Lawrence. And I'm scared to death of how I feel."

"For all the years I've known you, you've never allowed yourself to be human, to need anyone. You've turned into some kind of ice man without feelings. But Shannon's melted you, and now you're finding out what it means to be truly alone."

"You're wrong, Lawrence, there was a girl once. I loved her and she was taken from me."

"And she's gone, she's been gone for nearly twenty years. You told me once, when you were drunk. Then you passed out and never mentioned it again. That was young love, first love. Are you going to kill yourself out of regret? I thought you had more fortitude."

Jonathan swore and stood. "No, no, I'm not. I'm going after Shannon—for me. Find her, Lawrence."

• • •

But Lawrence didn't find her.

Christmas Eve came, and Jonathan put out the Santa Claus gifts. The next morning DeeDee examined what she found under the tree and seemed content with what she'd received. But Jonathan didn't miss her continued glances through the window, and when she insisted that they wait to open their personal gifts, he knew that he had to hurt her with the truth.

"She isn't coming, DeeDee," Jonathan said.

"Don't worry, Daddy, I know that you think she won't be here. But I know she will."

For the first time in his life Jonathan didn't know what to say.

Finally after a listless meal of picked-at turkey and barely tasted dressing, Jonathan took DeeDee into the study and sat down near the tree. "I know that you're waiting for Shannon," he said, "but we knew when she came that she was a fairy. People can't keep fairies, they have to be free. She couldn't stay with us, even if she wanted to."

"But—"

"I know it hurts, but we were very lucky to have had her just for a while, and she left Kaseybelle behind to keep you company because she loves you very much. Now she has to move on. We have to be very brave and love each other, punkin."

"Oh, Daddy, I do love you. But I wanted you to have someone special to love you too."

"I don't need anybody but you. Now, let's open our gifts. I want to know what's in that funny-looking package that looks like a big *L*."

The joy had gone out of the day, but DeeDee

agreed, climbing down to hand him the gift Shannon had helped her wrap.

Jonathan untied the bow and let the paper fall away. "A boomerang," he said. "Just what I always wanted."

"You can throw it away, Daddy, and it will always come back to you."

He might have missed the meaning of DeeDee's present if he hadn't opened Shannon's gift next. Inside a small white box, intricately cast in polished pewter, was a tiny, perfectly carved possum.

"Oh, look, Daddy. Now I understand." DeeDee held up a magic wand that she'd just unwrapped. "It's from Shannon. It's magic. I know it. It's filled with Kaseybelle's magic dust. Oh, Daddy, don't be sad. Merry Christmas. I love you."

She took the wand and walked out of the room as fast as her uncertain legs could carry her, leaving Jonathan staring at the possum in his hand.

"Oh, Shannon," he whispered. "Why did you leave? Did you really want to go?"

As if she were standing beside him, he could almost hear her saucy, "Is that a question?" and his firm answer, "You betcha."

No matter how awful Christmas had been in the past, this one was the worst of Shannon's life. She'd taken a midnight flight back to Atlanta and spent the next week not answering her phone or the door.

"No, Willie, I'm sure. I don't want any company for New Year's Eve. I've rented a video and picked up Chinese food. I'll be fine."

She would be, Shannon told herself as she hung

up the phone. First she'd take a long, hot soak in the tub, with mountains of bubbles. No, not mountains. She'd had enough of mountains in her life. Just a small frothy hill of pink foam would do. In the living room she turned on the stereo loud enough so that she could hear the music in the bathroom.

Moments later she was sliding into the sweet-scented liquid, her hair pinned on top of her head in a wild mass of damp curls. Closing her eyes, she leaned back, resting her head on the edge of the tub. She wouldn't think about Jonathan Dream. She'd learned her lesson about the pain of freeing her heart to love.

When she'd left the mall, she'd known her life was over. For a time she'd known joy and happiness. But she'd simply borrowed it. It never had belonged to her.

Nothing in her life was real. She'd been fooling herself for so long, living a dream that she'd built from bits and pieces of fantasy.

She moved her toes and watched the water slosh back and forth, evaporating the bubbles. Once, Shannon Summers had been pushed from one place to another like those ripples, until she'd begun to gather up and hoard small segments of peace. Little by little she'd managed to construct a separate life for herself, a life without hurt, without demands, without pain.

And she'd burrowed herself inside the fantasy. Except that it wasn't real.

Now the bubble had burst. She'd known the intense emotion of loving a man without restraint, without regret. She'd had, for a few brief, happy weeks, a beautiful child who'd believed in her and needed her. And she'd had a home that had been a sanctuary from the outside world.

But most of all, she'd had Jonathan for one magic moment. She'd thought it was enough.

Except that she hadn't had him. Nobody had Jonathan, because he wasn't free. He was still haunted by his past, just as she was by hers.

The water cooled. The bubbles disappeared. Finally, her hair hanging in damp, curly wisps, she climbed out of the tub, dried herself with a soft pink towel, and reached for her robe. It was late. Her Chinese food was cold and she didn't have the desire to reheat it. And the thought of watching a movie alone was suddenly too depressing.

She pulled on her old familiar robe and thought of the burgundy one she'd left behind, leaning her face against her shoulder, freeing a quick, unwelcome fantasy. Jonathan was holding her, lifting her in his arms, and carrying her to his bed. She could feel the strong, hard planes of his body, the ruffle of his hair against her cheek, the touch of his lips on her forehead.

He'd thought he was so empty, and yet he was a man with so much to give. He'd thought that he was displeasing to the eye, when his scarred exterior only added to his powerful mystique. His dark sensuality was fueled by such energy that the very air was heated in his presence. Yet he was good and caring. And he'd thought he had his life under control, until his daughter had asked him for a future.

He'd been undone by her request. She'd asked for the one thing he could never give her.

Would Shannon ever be able to forget?

Could she ever get past what had happened?

Could she go back to the simple, protected life she'd made for herself—and survive?

From the bathroom she wandered into the small living room that had always been her haven. She'd planned every piece of furniture, every picture—placed it, loved it, treasured the security it brought. But tonight it was just furniture. The music ended and the clock began to chime. The year was ending too.

On the stroke of midnight the doorbell rang.

"Willie." She sighed. "Dear Willie. I told you not to come." But she was glad he had. He'd have his latest lover with him, a woman who'd be bewildered that her date had chosen to visit another woman on New Year's Eve. Shannon would reassure him and send him away. She couldn't let him sacrifice his life for hers, not anymore.

But suddenly she didn't want to be alone. She needed someone. Willie and whoever he brought along would fill the emptiness for one night.

She opened the door and gasped.

"Shannon."

"Jonathan!"

"I had to come. May I come in?"

"Why?"

"I don't know. I need to be here, Shannon. With you."

"Why?"

"Dammit, Shannon, let me in!"

His voice was tight and threatening. He was angry. She'd never heard this kind of desperation before. She couldn't turn him away. Slowly she stepped back, making a space for him to come in.

A space, a space in her home, in her life. She was inviting him into her world now, into the empty place he'd made her see.

"I know that I have no right to be here. I have no right to mess up your life with my pain. You're kind and good, and you don't deserve this. But I didn't know what else to do."

Jonathan strode into the room and stood in the center, dwarfing the small space with his size. He was bareheaded. His scarred face and black eye patch were exposed. He was wearing jeans and the familiar heavy jacket. His feet were covered with fur-lined boots, and his hair was falling free across his shoulders.

He looked . . . untamed.

"What's wrong, Jonathan?" She closed the door and walked closer, hesitant, yet drawn by his need.

"Everything. Everything in my life is wrong. You took the magic out of my life, out of DeeDee's life. She doesn't understand why you left."

"I couldn't stay, Jonathan. Give her time and your love. She's strong now. She'll survive."

"I don't know. I thought so. Even after she didn't get what she asked Santa for, once she opened your gift, she seemed happy. She said she understood what you wanted her to do."

"Understood what?"

"That you would come back. She sleeps with that magic wand every night, and she waits. I wait too."

"Oh, dear. I'm so sorry, Jonathan."

Shannon's soft voice cut through Jonathan's anguish. He allowed himself to look at her. She was so very beautiful. Standing there in the soft light, her fine golden hair turning into a halo around her face. It was obvious that she'd just come from her bath. Face flushed, eyes full of concern, she was magnificent.

And he'd lost her.

All because he'd been such a fool. But he'd had no choice.

"I want to tell you about my wife. Mona's dead now, Shannon, but she didn't die in the accident. For the past three years she hasn't known who she was or where she was. For me she was already dead, but her body lived, as a constant reminder of what I'd done. Three weeks ago the hospital called. She'd started to fade."

That was when Mrs. Butter had been so worried, when Shannon had found him in the study, when he'd tried desperately to send her away.

"She finally stopped breathing," he went on. "I buried her, privately, two days ago. I never loved her, Shannon, but she was my wife. And I kept the world from learning the truth, and DeeDee from hating her mother."

"Oh, Jonathan."

"I'll explain the truth someday to DeeDee, when she's older."

"And what will you tell her?"

"That her birth mother loved her very much."

"Her birth mother?"

"Shannon, DeeDee is a little girl. She doesn't need to carry around my emotional baggage. She deserves a normal life, with a father and a mother. You know what she asked Santa to bring her."

Shannon didn't answer. She couldn't. What was he saying? Why was he here? She wondered. Whatever the reason, it was tied up in his grief and his guilt.

"She asked for you, Shannon."

She still didn't answer.

"She wants you to be her mother. Didn't you want the same thing?"

"I did say that, but I didn't know what DeeDee had asked Santa for—not then."

"I see."

Jonathan unzipped his jacket and let it fall to the floor. He walked over to the mantle and studied the painting hanging over it, the painting of Kaseybelle and her imaginary Milky Way Land. "I thought that's why you ran away, that you didn't want me."

Shannon could hear her heart pounding in the silence. She was glad that Jonathan had turned his head. She didn't want him to see her face, read it, see how badly she was trembling.

"She wants you, Shannon, and I," he said in a tight, raspy voice, "I want to marry you."

"No, Jonathan. I can't go back. I can't take the pain again. No matter how much I care about DeeDee, I won't compound the problem by marrying you."

"I want you, Shannon. I need you."

But you don't love me, she thought. *You won't allow yourself to love anybody.* "Why?"

"What happened at the mall showed me that I'm ready to leave the castle, come back to the world. But I don't think I can do it alone. For so long I've felt empty, as if everything was dead inside me. Then you came into my life and I dared to believe that I was alive."

"I'm the wrong woman. I'm more private than you are. I have no courage. I can't function in the limelight."

"You don't have to. We'll stay in the castle, if that's what you want. You have your office there. It'll work. We'll make it work."

"No, Jonathan. You're right. DeeDee needs a regular home, in a regular neighborhood with friends and neighbors. I don't think I can provide that."

"I'll help you, Shannon. We'll help each other. I love you, Shannon Summers."

But his confession of love had come too late. She couldn't believe it. "No, that's wrong. Don't you see, Jonathan, we're both flawed. We're using each other to be strong. It won't work for me, but you have a chance to change. You're free."

"And you? Where are your chains? What's holding you back? I love you, Shannon Summers. I left the castle, flew here on a commercial flight under my own name, and took a taxi to your apartment, all without a single thought of hiding myself from view. Doesn't that tell you anything?"

Perhaps he honestly believed he loved her. Could it be possible? No, she'd learned long ago not to trust anybody who professed love, not even herself.

"Jonathan, I'm going to try to explain why I can never be who you want. I can't be depended on. I've never told anybody this, not even Willie. I'll let you down, just as I let my mother down. Love means that a person is there for you. I won't be."

"That's nonsense. You're the most trustworthy person I've ever known."

"No, there's something wrong with me, Jonathan. No matter how bad things were for my mother, she always came back to me. She depended on me. But the one time she needed me most, I left her. And she killed herself because of my weakness."

"Shannon, I know about your mother. I had Lawrence check on her. Sofia was a boozed-up has-been who played on the sympathy of the last person on this earth who'd allow her abuse, her daughter. You had nothing to do with her killing herself. She'd been doing that for years."

"Yes, but if I'd been there, it wouldn't have happened. I left. I told her that I'd had enough and I wasn't going to watch her destroy herself. I wanted a life of my own. And I ran away. I was a coward. I let her die, Jonathan."

"No, walking away was strength. Staying would have been weak. I know, Shannon. I just walked away from my guilt, and I've come for you. We need each other."

"You're wrong. Didn't I just walk away from DeeDee?"

"Shannon, stop punishing yourself. Please don't turn me away."

As he waited for her answer, Shannon felt an invisible weight shift inside her. He was right. It wasn't protection from hurt that had forced her to seal herself away from the world, it was guilt. The fantasy she'd created for a little girl had protected the child, but she wasn't a little girl anymore. Kaseybelle had been passed on to another child who needed an anchor in an uncertain world. But Shannon had retreated to the safety of her old life.

"Ever since I left you," Shannon said, "I've felt as if I'm drifting. I've lost my focus somehow, and nothing seems quite right."

"I know." Jonathan took a step toward her, caught sight of her panicky expression, and stopped.

"I never asked for anything in my life, except for someone to care about me. That's why I created Kasey, my imaginary friend."

"And I created the DreamGirls. Not because I was lonely, but because I'd been hurt. The company and my life-style were the proof of my success, my armor against failure. But we were only fooling ourselves, Shannon."

He was right. She didn't need an imaginary fairy. Life had its own rewards, if she were willing to reach for them. And she wasn't alone, unless she chose to be. Looking at Jonathan's stern face, lined with worry, she understood that he was hurting for her now.

And he'd come for her, offering to be her strength, asking her to be his strength.

"Yes. We were deluding ourselves," she answered. "And if I reach out for you now, Jonathan, I'll be using you, just as I used Kasey. And you'll be using me too."

"You won't come back with me?"

"No, I can't."

"Don't you care that I love you?"

"Oh, yes. Never think I don't. But love isn't enough. Love only gives us the power to hurt. To survive that hurt, we have to find our own strength."

Jonathan let out a low curse and gritted his teeth. "And you think you have a monopoly on martyrdom. Well, you don't. I've carried my own load. But the difference between you and me is that eventually I got smart."

"I'm happy for you, Jonathan."

"Yeah, that and a buck will buy a cheap beer. Thanks, Shannon. If you change your mind, let me know. DeeDee set her mind on having a wedding on the mountain. She made Lawrence leave the Christmas star. It's going to be the first one on the Milky Way. All the Chocolate Sprinkles will be there."

Shannon couldn't speak.

"Too bad," he whispered, "too bad the bride won't be there."

Shannon heard the door slam. She felt the emptiness pressing against her like a physical presence, forcing the air from her lungs and enlarging the lump in her throat until she could barely breathe.

He'd come for her, and she'd let him leave.

This time the pain was unbearable.

"What did she say, Daddy? Did you ask her to marry us?"

"She said no, DeeDee."

The child's face fell, her lower lip began to quiver as she bravely held back the tears.

"But I did everything she said. I worked hard and I walked right up to Santa's North Pole. I sat on his knee and I told him what I wanted for Christmas, more than anything else in the world."

"I know, punkin. Santa Claus can bring us things, but sometimes he can't change people. They have to make their own choices, and no matter how hard we might want something, it doesn't always work out."

"Then I held Kaseybelle and wished with the magic wand. What else can we do?"

"Nothing, punkin."

"Maybe I could ask her? I'm sure if I asked her, she'd change her mind. Will you take me to Atlanta, Daddy, to see Shannon?"

"No, DeeDee. If Shannon wants us, she'll come. But we can't wait for her, we have to get on with our lives. Would you like to take a trip someplace?"

"No, I don't think so, Daddy. I think I'll go to bed

now. Tell Lawrence that I guess he can take down the star."

DeeDee slipped out of Jonathan's lap and stood, balancing herself carefully before she began to walk slowly out the door. There was still a noticeable limp, but that would lessen in time.

His daughter was walking, and that was all he'd started out to accomplish. But along the way a lithe, golden-haired beauty had touched their lives with fairy dust, just for a moment, and the world had become bright.

He turned his chair to the window and gazed out at the silver star hanging in the trees, his mind shifting back to another afternoon, when they'd donned Russian costumes and created a fantasy world in which they could love without regret.

Jonathan touched the scar on his face.

He'd fallen in love with the fantasy, and there was no way he could make it real.

Ten

For the next few days Shannon dragged herself to her desk, but Kaseybelle, the Kissy Chocolate Fairy, had lost her charm.

The cartoon episode dealing with Kaseybelle's fear in spending the night in a strange place aired, but Shannon knew the writers had missed the point. It wasn't meant to focus on Kaseybelle's conquering her fear of the dark because she was a fairy, it was to have centered on Kasey's finding the strength inside herself to do it without fairy magic.

The strength she wished she could find.

Willie flung himself into the NightDream account—literally. He even suggested that his newly hired staff members surround themselves with the products at home and in the office.

If the world had thought Willie bizarre before, Shannon wondered what they'd think about secretaries and a creative staff who wore the garments to work?

The next Kaseybelle television story idea was

due Monday, and Shannon had no idea what she'd suggest. It was Saturday morning when she ripped the last printout into shreds and added it to the others in the wastepaper basket beside her computer.

Happy thoughts and magic refused to flow. Instead she allowed herself to type the blackness that had smothered Kaseybelle's joy. Perhaps if she could get through her own darkness, she could erase the dark mood of the fairy.

Kaseybelle was to meet her new friend, Deanna, by the castle bridge. They were going to capture starfish for the new pond Deanna's father was building behind the castle. But Kaseybelle was late. First she stopped to help the chocolate ants who were gathering nutmeats for the winter. Then she happened on a mint leaf scheduled to flavor the latest batch of after-dinner candies. It had been caught up in a starstorm of fairy dust and blown out of the kitchen. Kaseybelle took the time to return the mint.

When she finally arrived at the castle bridge, Deanna was gone. But she'd cried so many tears that the pond had overflowed, washing all the fish they'd already captured over the side and leaving them to wither on the ground.

"Kaseybelle, you're just like me," Shannon snapped, "never there when you should be."

But that's not true, Kaseybelle argued back. *I helped the ants and the mint leaves, just like you helped DeeDee.*

"But—but—"

No more buts, Kaseybelle admonished sternly. *Sometimes we can't know that we're right. We just have to do what we think we ought to and believe in the magic. You've let yourself stop believing, Shannon.*

"There is no magic. Magic is an illusion, meant to deceive."

Kaseybelle was persistent. *What about Jonathan? What you two shared was magic, wasn't it?*

"Oh, yes, that was magic," Shannon typed. "But magic isn't real. Sofia found that out."

Sofia stopped believing too. But you can change things, if you believe that magic is the love in your heart.

Shannon sprang to her feet.

Magic is the love in your heart.

She was carrying on a conversation with her alter ego, and Kaseybelle was making more sense than her creator. So she had punished herself for her mistakes; she didn't have to repeat them. Just as Jonathan didn't have to repeat his.

Listen to what's in your heart.

Believe.

Quickly Shannon began to pack, then abandoned that idea. All she had to do was hurry. She suddenly felt a great sense of urgency. Grabbing her coat and her purse, she made plans. She'd hail a cab and catch the next flight to North Carolina.

She heard the phone ringing as she closed the door. But she didn't go back. Whatever it was could wait. Nothing was as important as getting to the mountain.

"Shannon isn't answering at home either, Lawrence."

"Where can she be? Willie says she's been

keeping herself away from everybody and everything."

"I don't know, but I'm not waiting here any longer. To hell with what the police said about staying here in case she comes back or calls. I can't believe that DeeDee thought she could just walk out the door and find her way to Shannon."

"We don't know that's where she's gone. Her note just said that she wasn't going to be afraid. She'd find Kaseybelle and believe in the magic."

"Kaseybelle! That's it, Lawrence. She made a lunch. She took Hap. She's gone to find Shannon. She's out there somewhere. For nearly three hours she's been out there. I'm going to join the search."

"Jonathan, half the law enforcement officials in the county are already looking for DeeDee. They have mounted an organized, systematic search. You'll just go off half-cocked, and next we'll be looking for you."

"Suppose she made it to the road and someone picked her up? Get me that television reporter, the one from the mall. Have him broadcast it on the air."

"You want me to invite the press up here?"

"I'll bring in that reporter and let him interview me personally if it will help us find DeeDee. Lawrence, it's getting dark. Suppose she's hurt, afraid?"

"They'll find her, Jonathan."

"Dammit, this wouldn't have happened if I'd brought Shannon back."

Shannon wasn't certain that a cab driver would attempt the drive up the mountain, but her promise of double fare solved the problem. She didn't know how she'd get through the locked gates, either, but she'd figure that out when she got there.

At the base of the mountain there were police cars and rescue vehicles with lights flashing and communication equipment squawking.

"What's wrong, driver? Stop and ask. Has there been an accident?"

He didn't have to stop, an officer flagged him down with his flashlight. "Where you headed, buddy."

Shannon answered for him. "Officer, I'm trying to get up the mountain. What's happened?"

"There's a little girl missing. We're searching for her."

"What little girl?" Shannon felt the blood in her veins turn to ice. "What little girl?"

"Jonathan Dream's daughter. Do you know anything about it?"

"DeeDee, oh no! Please let us pass. I have to get up there."

"Your name, ma'am?"

"Shannon Summers. Please, let me through."

A quick check on his portable phone and he waved the cab through the blockade.

Through the woods, on either side of the road, Shannon could see the men with flashlights moving back and forth. The gate was open. At the castle Lawrence met the cab, opened the door, and pulled Shannon to her feet. "I'm glad you're here," he said. "See if you can stop Jonathan from self-destructing. I'll take care of the cab driver."

Jonathan was in the study, staring out the window, his head leaning against the glass. Such wretched despair. Such aloneness. Such heavy pain.

"Jonathan?"

He turned slowly. He hadn't shaved, his heavy five-o'clock shadow covering his scowling face with blackness. His wild gaze slammed against her, taking her breath away and leaving her heart without its beat. She stumbled from the force of his fury.

"Why are you here?"

"I came because—because I—because you were right."

"Right? Fine. But you're too late. It doesn't matter anymore, unless DeeDee managed to find you and you've brought her home."

"Too late? No, that can't be."

Jonathan watched her as she visibly gathered her courage and straightened up to the full height of her slight figure. What was he doing, punishing the woman he loved because his daughter loved her too?

"No, Jonathan," she said, and took a step toward him. "You made me face myself and see that I wasn't responsible for my mother. I was there for her for all those years. When I left her, it was because it was time."

"Like you left us?"

Jonathan wished he could call the words back. Destroying Shannon wasn't what he wanted to do. But he didn't seem to be able to stop himself.

"Like I left you. But I know now that I have choices I didn't have with Sofia. I can choose to be here, choose to take a chance. And you gave me the courage to choose, Jonathan, you and DeeDee."

"Just like you gave DeeDee the courage to believe she could have the thing she wanted most in the world. Then you took it away."

"I know. I was wrong. That's what I came to say."

"Oh, and what is that?"

"I love you, Jonathan. I want to be with you. Here, or anyplace else in the world. Nobody can create a fantasy world, Jonathan. Not even us."

"Try telling that to DeeDee. She believed in your magic so much that she decided to go and find you. She's gone, Shannon. Gone! Try waving that magic wand of yours and see if you can find her. We can't."

The man standing before her wasn't the Jonathan who cut down the tree. He wasn't the man who'd taken his two favorite girls to Fantasy World to ride the carousel. This man was the angry barbarian who slayed his enemies and fed them to the lions. He'd finally become the Phantom of the Opera, and he was being destroyed by his love.

Until she saw what he was working through his fingers.

The tiny, carved, pewter possum. He was holding it there in the shadows, in the light of the fire, staring at her with the stark need of a man who was dying.

"Oh, Jonathan," she whispered, and held out her arms. "Please, I love you. We need each other. I've come home. Let's not hurt each other anymore."

And then she was in his arms and felt his trembling. She didn't know who started crying first, and she didn't care. They cleansed the hate and kindled mutual comfort as they held each other without speaking. Too many words had been said. They'd forgotten the magic of allowing themselves to feel. Now it came slowly back, thawing the ice, forging two beings into one.

Until at last Jonathan pulled back, lifting her head. "I'm sorry," he whispered. "I was so afraid that I just struck out. I never meant to hurt you."

"I know."

"No, you don't. You never believed me when I told you that I'd hurt you. I always hurt people."

"Only because you love them. Love gives us the power to hurt and be hurt. It also gives us the courage to start again. We have to find DeeDee now, Jonathan. Then we'll find us."

He kissed her, softly, gently, making the kiss a promise.

"Now," she said, pulling away. "Tell me exactly what happened."

"Well, she'd been pretty quiet for a few days. Mrs. Butterfield said she was watching that television program about Kaseybelle spending the night in her friend Deanna's castle. Afterward she seemed preoccupied."

"And—what made you think she was coming to me?"

"She told Mrs. Butterfield. Though she didn't know what DeeDee meant at the time. It was only later that we put it together."

Shannon took off her coat and moved toward the fire. "What exactly did she tell Mrs. Butter?"

"She said that all she had to do was be like Kaseybelle. If she wasn't afraid of the dark, the magic would make everything all right.

"It didn't make any sense to Mrs. Butterfield. DeeDee isn't afraid of the dark. It was the next statement that finally got through. She said that she wasn't afraid any more. All she had to do now was wait for you. If you didn't come, she'd go and get you, even if Daddy didn't want her to."

"But what makes you think she went to find me?"

"The missing food. She packed a lunch. And she took Happy. We haven't been able to find either of them since early afternoon."

Shannon stared into the flames. "There has to be some connection between DeeDee's disappearance and the Kissy Chocolate television program. She said she would learn not to be afraid anymore?"

"That's what Butter said. But she thought she was talking about her legs."

"No, that's what Kaseybelle said in the program. She went to the castle tower to conquer her fear of the dark. The power of her magic helped her to be very brave, for which she was given a reward."

"What does that have to do—"

"The tower room. Jonathan, have you searched the turret where I stayed?"

"I—I don't know. Mrs. Butter and Lawrence searched, but DeeDee can't get up there. Her legs are getting stronger, but she'd never make that climb."

Shannon sprang to her feet. "Oh, yes, she would. That's how she intended to conquer her fear. Come on."

She ran down the corridor to the main steps, reached the second floor, and headed for the tower.

"But what about Happy? We've called and called. He would have answered."

"Not if he's in the tower. It's practically soundproof. He wouldn't hear you."

"God, I hope you're right."

At the door Shannon paused, took a deep breath, and reached for Jonathan's hand. If she were wrong and the room was empty, she didn't think she could survive. "Don't let her know how worried you were, Jonathan."

The door opened to a room drawn in shadows. Happy padded over and gave both Jonathan and Shannon a wet, slurpy greeting before wandering through the door and down the stairs.

"She's here, Shannon. Look, in the bed."

DeeDee was sleeping, her tearstained face relaxed in innocent dreams. Beside her lay the Kaseybelle doll and in her hand was the magic wand that Shannon had given her for Christmas.

Shannon felt Jonathan's arm slide around her, and she laid her head on his shoulder. She knew what it meant to feel peace as they stood, united, looking down at the child.

Then DeeDee opened her eyes, her lips curving into a broad smile.

"I knew you'd come," she said. "I loved you here."

"I know," Shannon said, "I felt it."

"And you aren't going to leave us, are you?"

"Absolutely not, never again."

Jonathan lifted DeeDee into his arms.

"Daddy, look out the window. Look at all the lights. Fairy lights. It's the Milky Way, here on our mountain. I knew it all along."

Dinner was a joyous affair. DeeDee explained in great detail to Lawrence about Milky Way Land, about the fairy lights. "That's the way it will be when we get married," she said with authority. "Won't it, Daddy?"

"Hey, I think we ought to ask our bride, don't you?"

But he didn't have to ask. Throughout dinner he'd felt the tingling return, the warmth of the connection reestablish itself. If the linkage became any more pronounced, they'd probably glow in the dark. And DeeDee would think that it was part of the magic.

Jonathan had sent the searchers away. He'd even agreed to a televised interview by Noel Cross, where he thanked all the people who'd come to help. In a surprise gesture he also announced that the castle in the background was going to be reproduced in the valley below and turned into a center for the treatment of trauma victims. It would be called the Magic Through Love Miracle Center, established in the name of Mona Drew.

Finally, when DeeDee's eyelids began to droop, Mrs. Butterfield suggested it was time for bed. She walked DeeDee toward the door, where the little girl stopped.

"You were right, Shannon. All you have to do is believe and you'll get what you want most in the whole world. But sometimes it isn't easy."

Afterward, in the study, Jonathan took his coffee and walked toward the window. "She's right, sometimes it isn't easy."

Shannon came to stand beside him. There was an awkwardness between them that hadn't been there before. "You're right. But anything worth having is worth fighting for."

"Can we make it, Shannon? Can we get beyond the fantasy, the magic, and live in the real world?"

"Definitely not."

He put down his cup and turned to face her. "What does that mean?"

"I've done a lot of thinking since I left here, Jonathan, about magic and fantasies."

"So have I."

"I believe that I've figured out the answer. All magic has as its foundation one thing that makes it possible. Without it, the magic would never be believed."

"What's that?"

"It's very simple. The fantasy of magic is love. People who don't have the capacity for love don't believe in magic. I created Kaseybelle because I needed love. I believed in her for love. She is the love that kept me safe for you."

"How do you explain me? I never believed in anything, certainly not love. Love's brought me the deepest hurt and the darkest lows."

"We wouldn't appreciate the light if we didn't have darkness, Jonathan. Love can only grow when we let it. You made your own world to protect you, to keep you and DeeDee safe for me."

Jonathan thought he'd never seen such beauty as in Shannon standing beside him, looking up at him with trust and acceptance. She was giving him her love without demands, without reservation. Could it really be that simple?

"Is *love* another word for 'magic'?" he asked, taking her hand.

"Oh, yes, and magic is forever."

And then he kissed her. It was a gentle, giving kiss. Jonathan Dream would never be able to conceal emotions once freed. Like the detonation of a dam, the full force of his intensity and passion swept over her, propelling her beyond the mountaintop.

"Do you love me, Shannon Summers?"

"Is that a question?" she asked breathlessly.

"You betcha." He lifted her in his arms and carried her up the stairs.

"Where are you taking me?"

"Where else? The Milky Way." He climbed the turret steps, pressing her against him, planting fiery little kisses across her forehead and along her cheek. The fire zigzagged down her body, fusing with the blaze being fed by his fingertips until she felt as if she were imploding. Inside the room he let her down, unbuttoning buttons, flinging clothes behind them until they were both naked. The only light was that of the moon, streaming through the windows. The only heat was the heat they created with their need.

"You'll always be magic to me," he whispered, as he placed her on the bed.

"I want to be," she answered, studying him in the moonlight. "This had to be a fantasy, my being loved by a scarred warlock, a night vision, a phantom who is too savage to be real."

"I'll have the scars repaired. I don't need them anymore."

"No, don't," she said, "I like them. They're part of you. And you're a part of me."

And then he was. They didn't go slow. Her arms were around his neck and her legs were around his waist. He was plunging inside her, joining with her, branding her with his need and searing her with his essence. Together they began to tremble. Together they died and survived, each knowing that this moment would never come again. Yet each becoming the other's courage.

• • •

Snow covered the mountain. Lighted stars hung from every tree limb, turning the snow into a moving kaleidoscope of color. The world was a jeweled fairyland for the wedding of Jonathan Dream and Shannon Summers.

Jonathan created Shannon's wedding gown. He took the gold from the sun and the silver from the moon, spinning an illusion that made her an angel. DeeDee, wearing a matching dress that covered her almost-discarded braces, led the bridal procession down the grand staircase, dropping silver flowers and golden leaves before them.

At the bottom of the stairway beneath a golden arch was Jonathan.

With his dark hair flowing roguishly across his shoulders and the devilish patch covering his eye, Jonathan looked every inch the Turkish king his blue-satin jacket had been made for. As Shannon came to stand beside him, he held out his hand. Once they touched, he knew that the magic was there. The love he felt for this woman who'd filled his life with joy was not a fantasy.

The minister said the words, and they responded. After the ceremony the minister announced that they were man and wife, Mr. and Mrs. Jonathan Drew, and Mr. Drew could kiss the bride.

"Mrs. Drew?" Shannon asked with lifted eyebrows.

"Of course, the only dream we'll ever need is the fantasy we share."

Willie, Mrs. Butterfield, and Lawrence watched as a shower of silver fell from somewhere above, covering the bride and groom and DeeDee with stardust.

But Jonathan and Shannon didn't need the illusion. They carried their magic in their hearts. The stardust was only the visible expression of the promise of forever.

Beyond the castle the night sky provided a royal velvet canopy above the twinkling stars. Then the snow began to fall, large, lacy flakes that turned the mountain once more into a wonderland.

"Look, Jonathan, it's snowing."

"I'm sorry, darling. Looks like we won't be able to leave right away for that trip to Paris."

"So, we'll stay right here, in our magic place. Will you mind?"

"No," he said, lifting her in his arms. "The only honeymoon I want is here, with you."

"By the way," he asked later as they lay entwined in each other's arms in the turret room, languishing in the afterglow, "when are you going to tell me about the possums?"

"Oh, that's a tale for another time," she whispered, sliding her body over his. "Will you wait?"

"Is that a question, wife?"

Wife.

Mother.

The promise of forever.

"You betcha," she said.

THE EDITOR'S CORNER

What could be more romantic than Valentine's Day and six LOVESWEPT romances all in one glorious month! Celebrate this special time of the year by cuddling up with the wonderful books coming your way soon.

The first of our reading treasures is **ANGELS SINGING** by Joan Elliott Pickart, LOVESWEPT #594. Drew Sloan's first impression of Memory Lawson isn't the best, considering she's pointing a shotgun at him and accusing him of trespassing on her mountain. But the heat that flashes between them convinces him to stay and storm the walls around her heart . . . until she believes that she's just the kind of warm, loving woman he's been looking for. Joan comes through once more with a winning romance!

We have a real treat in store for fans of Kay Hooper. After a short hiatus for work on **THE DELANEY CHRISTMAS CAROL** and other books, Kay returns with **THE TOUCH OF MAX,** LOVESWEPT #595, the *fiftieth* book in her illustrious career! If you were a fan of Kay's popular "Hagan Strikes Again" and "Once Upon a Time" series, you'll be happy to know that **THE TOUCH OF MAX** is the first of four "Men of Mysteries Past" books, all of which center around Max Bannister's priceless gem collection, which the police are using as bait to catch a notorious thief. But when innocent Dinah Layton gets tangled in the trap, it'll take that special touch of Max to set her free . . . and capture her heart. A sheer delight—and it'll have you breathlessly waiting for more. Welcome back, Kay!

In Charlotte Hughes's latest novel, Crescent City's new soccer coach is **THE INCREDIBLE HUNK,** LOVESWEPT #596. Utterly male, gorgeously virile, Jason Profitt has the magic touch with kids. What more perfect guy could there be for a redhead with five children to raise! But Maggie Farnsworth is sure that once he's seen her chaotic life, he'll run for the hills. Jason has another plan of action in mind, though—to make a home in her loving arms. Charlotte skillfully blends humor and passion in this page-turner of a book.

Appropriately enough, Marcia Evanick's contribution to the month, **OVER THE RAINBOW,** LOVESWEPT #597, is set in a small town called Oz, where neither Hillary Walker nor Mitch Ferguson suspects his kids of matchmaking when he's forced to meet the lovely speech teacher. The plan works so well the kids are sure they'll get a mom for Christmas. But Hillary has learned never to trust her heart again, and only Mitch's passionate persuasion can change her mind. You can count on Marcia to deliver a fun-filled romance.

A globetrotter in buckskins and a beard, Nick Leclerc has never considered himself **THE FOREVER MAN,** LOVESWEPT #598, by Joan J. Domning. Yet when he appears in Carla Hudson's salon for a haircut and a shave, her touch sets his body on fire and fills him with unquenchable longing. The sexy filmmaker has leased Carla's ranch to uncover an ancient secret, but instead he finds newly awakened dreams of hearth and home. Joan will capture your heart with this wonderful love story.

Erica Spindler finishes this dazzling month with **TEMPTING CHANCE,** LOVESWEPT #599. Shy Beth Waters doesn't think she has what it takes to light the sensual spark in gorgeous Chance Michaels. But the outrageous results of her throwing away a chain letter finally convince her that she's woman enough to tempt Chance—and that he's more than eager to be caught in her embrace. Humorous, yet seething with emotion and desire, **TEMPTING CHANCE** is one tempting morsel from talented Erica.

Look for four spectacular novels on sale now from FANFARE. Award-winning Iris Johansen confirms her place as a major star with **THE TIGER PRINCE,** a magnificent new historical romance that sweeps from exotic realms to the Scottish highlands. In a locked room of shadows and sandalwood, Jane Barnaby meets adventurer Ruel McClaren and is instantly transformed from a hard-headed businesswoman to the slave of a passion she knows she must resist.

Suzanne Robinson first introduced us to Blade in **LADY GALLANT,** and now in the new thrilling historical romance **LADY DEFIANT,** Blade returns as a bold, dashing hero. One of Queen Elizabeth's most dangerous spies, he must romance a beauty named Oriel who holds a clue that could change history. Desire builds and sparks fly as these two unwillingly join forces to thwart a deadly conspiracy.

Hailed by Katherine Stone as "emotional, compelling, and triumphant!", **PRIVATE SCANDALS** is the debut novel by very talented Christy Cohen. From the glamour of New York to the glitter of Hollywood comes a heartfelt story of scandalous desires and long-held secrets . . . of dreams realized and longings denied . . . of three remarkable women whose lifelong friendship would be threatened by one man.

Available once again is **A LOVE FOR ALL TIME** by bestselling author Dorothy Garlock. In this moving tale, Casey Farrow gives up all hope of a normal life when a car crash leaves indelible marks on her breathtaking beauty . . . until Dan Farrow, the man who rescued her from the burning vehicle, convinces her that he loves her just the way she is.

Also on sale this month in the hardcover edition from Doubleday is **THE LADY AND THE CHAMP** by Fran Baker. When a former Golden Gloves champion meets an elegant, uptown girl, the result is a stirring novel of courageous love that Julie Garwood has hailed as "unforgettable."

Happy reading!

With warmest wishes,

Nita Taublib

Nita Taublib
Associate Publisher
LOVESWEPT and FANFARE

OFFICIAL RULES TO WINNERS CLASSIC SWEEPSTAKES

No Purchase necessary. To enter the sweepstakes follow instructions found elsewhere in this offer. You can also enter the sweepstakes by hand printing your name, address, city, state and zip code on a 3" x 5" piece of paper and mailing it to: Winners Classic Sweepstakes, P.O. Box 785, Gibbstown, NJ 08027. Mail each entry separately. Sweepstakes begins 12/1/91. Entries must be received by 6/1/93. Some presentations of this sweepstakes may feature a deadline for the Early Bird prize. If the offer you receive does, then to be eligible for the Early Bird prize your entry must be received according to the Early Bird date specified. Not responsible for lost, late, damaged, misdirected, illegible or postage due mail. Mechanically reproduced entries are not eligible. All entries become property of the sponsor and will not be returned.

Prize Selection/Validations: Winners will be selected in random drawings on or about 7/30/93, by VENTURA ASSOCIATES, INC., an independent judging organization whose decisions are final. Odds of winning are determined by total number of entries received. Circulation of this sweepstakes is estimated not to exceed 200 million. Entrants need not be present to win. All prizes are guaranteed to be awarded and delivered to winners. Winners will be notified by mail and may be required to complete an affidavit of eligibility and release of liability which must be returned within 14 days of date of notification or alternate winners will be selected. Any guest of a trip winner will also be required to execute a release of liability. Any prize notification letter or any prize returned to a participating sponsor, Bantam Doubleday Dell Publishing Group, Inc., its participating divisions or subsidiaries, or VENTURA ASSOCIATES, INC. as undeliverable will be awarded to an alternate winner. Prizes are not transferable. No multiple prize winners except as may be necessary due to unavailability, in which case a prize of equal or greater value will be awarded. Prizes will be awarded approximately 90 days after the drawing. All taxes, automobile license and registration fees, if applicable, are the sole responsibility of the winners. Entry constitutes permission (except where prohibited) to use winners' names and likenesses for publicity purposes without further or other compensation.

Participation: This sweepstakes is open to residents of the United States and Canada, except for the province of Quebec. This sweepstakes is sponsored by Bantam Doubleday Dell Publishing Group, Inc. (BDD), 666 Fifth Avenue, New York, NY 10103. Versions of this sweepstakes with different graphics will be offered in conjunction with various solicitations or promotions by different subsidiaries and divisions of BDD. Employees and their families of BDD, its division, subsidiaries, advertising agencies, and VENTURA ASSOCIATES, INC., are not eligible.

Canadian residents, in order to win, must first correctly answer a time limited arithmetical skill testing question. Void in Quebec and wherever prohibited or restricted by law. Subject to all federal, state, local and provincial laws and regulations.

Prizes: The following values for prizes are determined by the manufacturers' suggested retail prices or by what these items are currently known to be selling for at the time this offer was published. Approximate retail values include handling and delivery of prizes. Estimated maximum retail value of prizes: 1 Grand Prize ($27,500 if merchandise or $25,000 Cash); 1 First Prize ($3,000); 5 Second Prizes ($400 each); 35 Third Prizes ($100 each); 1,000 Fourth Prizes ($9.00 each) ; 1 Early Bird Prize ($5,000); Total approximate maximum retail value is $50,000. Winners will have the option of selecting any prize offered at level won. Automobile winner must have a valid driver's license at the time the car is awarded. Trips are subject to space and departure availability. Certain black-out dates may apply. Travel must be completed within one year from the time the prize is awarded. Minors must be accompanied by an adult. Prizes won by minors will be awarded in the name of parent or legal guardian.

For a list of Major Prize Winners (available after 7/30/93): send a self-addressed, stamped envelope entirely separate from your entry to: Winners Classic Sweepstakes Winners, P.O. Box 825, Gibbstown, NJ 08027. Requests must be received by 6/1/93. DO NOT SEND ANY OTHER CORRESPONDENCE TO THIS P.O. BOX.

SWP 9/92

FANFARE

On Sale in December

THE TIGER PRINCE

☐ 29968-9 $5.50/6.50 in Canada

by Iris Johansen

Bantam's "Mistress of Romantic Fantasy"
author of THE GOLDEN BARBARIAN

LADY DEFIANT

☐ 29574-8 $4.99/5.99 in Canada

by Suzanne Robinson

Bestselling author of LADY GALLANT
and LADY HELLFIRE

"Lavish in atmosphere, rich in adventure, filled with suspense and passion, LADY DEFIANT is a fitting sequel to LADY GALLANT. Suzanne Robinson brilliantly captures the era with all the intrigue, costume, drama, and romance that readers adore." --*Romantic Times*

PRIVATE SCANDALS

☐ 56053-0 $4.99//5.99 in Canada

by Christy Cohen

A stunning debut novel of friendship,
betrayal, and passionate romance

A LOVE FOR ALL TIME

☐ 29996-4 $4.50/5.50 in Canada

by Dorothy Garlock

One of Ms. Garlock's most beloved romances of all time

Ask for these books at your local bookstore or use this page to order.

☐ Please send me the books I have checked above. I am enclosing $ ______ (add $2.50 to cover postage and handling). Send check or money order, no cash or C. O. D.'s please.

Name ____________________

Address ____________________

City/ State/ Zip ____________________

FANFARE

Send order to: Bantam Books, Dept. FN89, 2451 S. Wolf Rd., Des Plaines, IL 60018
Allow four to six weeks for delivery.
Prices and availability subject to change without notice.

FN89 1/93